From the Files of

Madison Finn

Read all the books about Madison Finn!

Coming soon!

Don't miss the Super Edition

From the Files of

Madison Finn

On the Case

By Laura Dower

HYPERION

New York

Text copyright © 2004 by Laura Dower

From the Files of Madison Finn and the Volo colophon are trademarks of Disney Enterprises, Inc.
Volo® is a registered trademark of Disney Enterprises, Inc.

Printed in the United States of America

First Edition
1 3 5 7 9 10 8 6 4 2

The main body of text in this book is set in 13-point Frutiger Roman.

ISBN 0-7868-0987-6

Visit www.hyperionbooksforchildren.com

For Myles and Olivia

Chapter 1

"Phinnie, move! You're blocking the screen."

Madison Finn reached into the blue ceramic bowl on her lap and munched another handful of popcorn.

"Mmmphinnnn!" she mumbled, trying to shoo her pug away from his inconvenient seat directly in front of the television set. She quickly stood up and gave Phin a nudge with her foot.

Nothing could get in the way of watching *Crime Time* every Friday night; this was especially true for the beginning of the show, when host Major DeMille did his introduction and presented the Case of the Week. Each *Crime Time* episode featured reenactments of crimes, with actors in the roles of attackers, victims, and so on. But Major DeMille was the major attraction. Madison even had downloaded his photograph to use as one of her screen savers—when she wasn't using one of her favorite animal photos.

"Are you going to have any more of this dinner?" Mom asked. She strolled into the living room holding a plate of pasta salad.

Madison waved Mom off.

"Madison, put down the remote control and answer me," Mom said.

"Mom!" Madison cried. She threw her hands into the air. "I'm watching *Crime Time* right now. You know I've been waiting all week to see this new episode. Can't we talk later?"

"Well, do you want this food or—"

"No, thanks, I have popcorn."

Madison turned back to the TV and her post-dinner snack.

"Crime Time, huh?" Mom wrinkled her brow. "I don't know how I feel about all these crime shows, Maddie. You have been talking a lot about mysteries lately. And I know it's only eight-thirty and this should be considered okay viewing for a twelve-year-old, but still—"

"I'm almost thirteen, Mom," Madison said, correcting her. "Um, can we talk about this later? Please?"

Mom sighed and sat on the sofa. "What is so interesting about this show?"

"Mommm!"

Madison settled back onto the sofa and turned the volume up so that her mom wouldn't interrupt her again. Phin jumped onto the couch and curled up at Madison's side.

Welcome to a place where crimes are stopped dead in their tracks . . . where the only way out is justice . . . where anytime is Crime Time.

Major DeMille's blond head filled the screen. Madison swooned. Major squinted as though he were staring right through the screen, into Madison's living room, and directly into her eyes.

The police have already surveyed the scene. But there are still many questions. Questions that no one seems to know how to answer . . .

"Isn't he dreamy?" Madison asked aloud. She grabbed another handful of popcorn.

"Who? That guy in the leather coat?" Mom asked.

Madison shot a look in Mom's direction. "Are you kidding? Mom, that is Major DeMille. He is only the hottest crime fighter ever."

"He solves the crimes?" Mom asked. "But isn't he an actor? He's just the narrator, Maddie."

"Yeah, well . . ." Madison nodded. "Last week was 'Double-Cross My Heart,' an episode about this couple who disappeared. Major DeMille was right there with all the key evidence."

"Maddie!" Mom said, rolling her eyes. "How can you watch this?"

Madison nodded. "Shhhh! They're coming to the best part."

Mom promptly stood up and clicked off the television.

"What did you do that for?" Madison asked frantically.

Mom crossed her arms in front of her chest. "Because," she said sternly, "I don't think this is the right thing for you to be watching."

"Mom!" Madison huffed. "Everyone watches this. It's fun to help solve the crimes."

"Oh, Maddie," Mom groaned. "Why don't you go read a book or something instead?"

"Mom, I finished my homework. What's the problem?"

"Madison . . ." Mom pursed her lips.

"Mommmmmmm," Madison whined.

"Oh, fine!" Mom threw up her arms. "Do what you want, Maddie."

She walked out of the living room and left Madison alone with the dog and the popcorn.

Half an hour later, Major DeMille reappeared to give his *Crime Time* recap. On-screen, faces flashed. People confessed. Police sirens wailed. The *Crime Time* gavel came crashing down.

Tune in for the next thrilling episode of Crime Time. . . .

Madison waited for the preview of next week's

show, which was titled "Bad and Badder," before she turned off the TV set.

"Hey! Mom!" she called out. "It's over now. Are you happy?"

But Mom wasn't listening anymore. She had the phone in her hand and a serious look on her face.

"What's wrong?" Madison asked as soon as Mom hung up the phone.

"That was Dad. Stephanie is in the hospital. She broke her wrist. Fell down when someone bumped into her on the street. He called to say that dinner tomorrow would have to be postponed."

"Wow," Madison said. "Is she going to be okay?"

"Yes, she'll be fine. She needs to wear a cast for a while. She's heading home tonight. Dad just wanted to let you know."

Madison realized that she was still holding on to the empty bowl of popcorn. She placed it in the sink and sat down at the kitchen table.

"Are you heading upstairs now?" Mom asked.

Madison nodded. "I have to get my beauty sleep. Besides, tomorrow I'm going to stay up later than late to watch part of the *Crime Time* marathon."

"A marathon?" Mom asked. "Sounds long."

Madison grinned. "Yeah. They're going to show the best twenty shows over and over, back to back, all weekend."

"But haven't you seen all of the episodes already?" Mom asked.

"Uh-huh. I think I've seen a couple of them five or six times," Madison said. "But Fiona hasn't seen any."

Fiona Waters was one of Madison's best friends. She lived right up the street and around the corner. They liked to spend as much time as possible at each other's houses.

"That's what you and Fiona are planning to do for your sleepover tomorrow? Watch television?" Mom said, sounding wary again.

"You should really watch, too, Mom," Madison said with a smile. "Major DeMille is showing 'The Talking Skull' and 'Footprints to Nowhere.' Those are some of the best *Crime Time* episodes ever."

"Whatever you say, Maddie," Mom said, rolling her eyes. "I'm sure you and Fiona will have a super time—without me."

Phin barked.

"And you, too, Phinnie," Mom said. "Can't forget you."

On Saturday night, Fiona arrived at Madison's house dragging her backpack and pillow behind her.

"Why didn't Aimee want to come to our sleepover?" Fiona asked Madison as she walked inside.

Aimee Gillespie was the other best friend in Madison and Fiona's trio of BFFs. She was also one of the best ballet dancers in the seventh grade—or any grade.

"Aimee thinks watching *Crime Time* is stupid," Madison explained. "She likes love stories more."

"Well, I can't *wait* to see it!" Fiona said excitedly. "I love scary stuff."

"It's not exactly scary," Madison explained. "More like mysterious. And Major DeMille is *hot*."

Fiona giggled. "Great."

Madison cracked up. "Not as hot as Egg, of course . . ."

Fiona elbowed Madison. She knew it was a joke. Fiona had been "going out" (at least that's what they called it) with one of Madison's best guy friends, Walter "Egg" Diaz, for a little while. At first, Madison had hated the idea of their dating, but she was getting used to it over time. Now she could even tease Fiona about it a little without hard feelings.

They grabbed the tuna sandwiches and fruit salad Mom had left them for dinner, along with a bowl of buttered popcorn, and headed into the living room to watch the show. That night's episode was based on recent events. It was called "The Masked Avenger."

Madison turned the lights down. The TV set cast a pale blue glow over the entire room.

Tonight we meet a robber who wears a different disguise for every robbery he commits. Last week, he broke into houses wearing a rabbit suit. Yesterday, he knocked off a bank wearing a red beard and a

patch over one eye. Tomorrow, who knows what he'll be wearing?

"A hula skirt," Fiona said, cracking up.

"Fiona, these are serious crimes," Madison insisted.

"Serious? In a rabbit suit?" Fiona said.

It *did* sound funny, but Madison was right. Despite the rather humorous disguises, this was one nasty robber, and he had committed one crime after another. He'd stolen more than two million dollars over four years, robbing banks and homes across the country.

Major DeMille's voice got very low as he stared into the camera. Madison stared back.

Will the Masked Avenger ever be caught? Will the Masked Avenger strike in your neighborhood next?

Madison flinched. *Her* neighborhood?

"Wait," Fiona said. "I heard my dad talking about this guy the other day. He robbed some banks in the next town. Don't you remember? Wow. That's a little close for comfort."

Cra-a-a-a-a-a-ack.

Madison's head spun around toward the window. "Did you hear that?" she asked, gripping the pillow on the sofa.

"Hear what?" Fiona said. "That was just the wind."

"Are you sure?" Madison asked.

Cra-a-a-a-a-a-ack.

"There it is again!" Madison said. She jumped up and peered through the window. "That was not the wind."

"I guess not," Fiona said. "It sounded like someone stepping on twigs or something."

Even Phinnie cowered behind a pillow on the sofa.

"Look!" Madison pointed to the scene outside the window. "It's a full moon tonight."

"Um, Maddie, you're scaring me," Fiona said.

Madison's voice got very low. "Fiona, are you thinking what I'm thinking?"

Fiona gulped. "The Masked Avenger?" she asked softly.

Knock-knock.

Madison and Fiona grabbed each other's hands and took deep breaths. The knock was at Madison's front door, just a few feet away from where they were sitting.

Madison clicked off the TV set. The room got very dark.

"Someone's out there," Madison whispered.

"Rowwwwwroooo," Phin moaned.

"Shhhhh! Be quiet, dog," Fiona said.

"There is no way the real Masked Avenger is outside right now," Madison said, trying to be calm.

They stared at the door. They didn't move.

"Madison?"

Mom came walking into the room. She clicked on the switch and flooded the room with light. "What are you two doing in the dark? Did someone knock at the door? I thought I heard a knock."

"Well," Madison stammered. "I—I—I think someone did . . . I don't know for sure. . . ."

Knock-knock.

"Maddie?" Mom smiled. "Are you expecting someone?"

"No," Madison shook her head. "Don't answer it, Mom."

"It could be the Masked Avenger," Fiona added.

"Girls!" Mom said, reaching for the knob. "I think you've had quite enough of *Crime Time*. Your imaginations are running wild."

Mom went to the door and started to open it. Phinnie waddled over, his tail between his legs. Even *he* was afraid of what would happen next.

"Surprise!" a voice cried out from the other side of the door.

Fiona and Madison both jumped backward onto the sofa, their hearts beating fast. "A-a-a-aaaaghhh!" they screamed at once.

"Maddie! Fiona!" Mom shrieked. "What's gotten into you girls?"

There in the doorway stood the mysterious visitor. But it wasn't the Masked Avenger. It was Aimee, with a sleeping bag and duffel.

"Oh, my God!" Aimee said. "Why did you scream

like that? I almost fell down your porch steps, Maddie."

"Aim?" Madison said.

"Are you joining the sleepover?" Mom asked.

Aimee shrugged. "I hope so," she said. "If Maddie and Fiona don't mind."

"I thought you said you didn't want to come over for the *Crime Time* marathon," Fiona said.

"Yeah, you said my favorite show was boring," Madison added.

"I know," Aimee said. "But I don't want to sit home alone. That's even more boring."

Aimee knelt down and scratched the top of Phin's head. His tail was wagging.

Fiona knelt, too, and threw her arms around Aimee.

"Are we ever glad to see you! We thought you were one of the escaped criminals from *Crime Time*," Fiona admitted.

"Huh? Escaped criminal? From a TV show?" Aimee said. "What are you talking about?"

"Long story," Madison said, a little embarrassed. "Want some popcorn?"

Chapter 2

 Crime Time

It's official. I watched episodes of
Crime Time on the marathon from Friday
until last night, and my eyes are sooooo
tired. But wow do I love that show! And I
LOVE MAJOR DEMILLE EVEN MORE!!!! He gets to
be more of a hottie with each new episode.
He's featured in this month's issue of Star
Beat too, and I am putting his picture on
my locker. Definitely.

Rude Awakening: Crime Time flies when
you're having fun.

Right now I'm up in the media lab at
school, between classes. We had a fire

drill just now and got released from second period a little early. I should be finishing up math homework, but I'm not. Instead, I have Crime Time on the brain. All I can think about are forensic DNA, footprints, and other evidence like what I saw on the show. Everything looks like some kind of clue to me. Like this chewed-up yellow pencil I see on the floor. Who does it belong to? Why is it there?

Someone was yelling in the locker room earlier today because she had her sneakers stolen during morning basketball practice. She should have yelled for me. I bet I could have found them.

Madison heard a noise behind her in the media lab. She pressed the SAVE button on her keyboard. The screen saver featuring Major DeMille popped up.

"Who is *that* turkey?" said the person behind her.

"Egg! Way to give me a heart attack!" Madison cried. She turned around to face her friend. "Do you always have to creep up on me like that when I'm at the computer?"

"Well, yeah. I like it when you jump," Egg said.

"I hate you sometimes," Madison said, poking him in the ribs.

"Drew and I were up here picking up a book. Want to walk to Mrs. Wing's class together?" Egg asked.

Drew waved from across the library.

"Sure. I'll walk with you," Madison said. She popped her disk out of the computer and stuffed it into her orange bag.

Luckily, the time in Mrs. Wing's computer lab zipped by. So did the rest of the day's classes. Madison even survived her third-period math class in spite of not having completed her homework. When the final bell of the day rang, Madison rushed to her locker.

"Look out!"

Madison stopped just before colliding with Hart Jones, her longtime crush at school.

"Hey, slow down, Finnster," Hart said, touching her arm. Lately, he'd been showing some serious signs that the crush might be mutual.

"Hi, Hart," Madison said quietly, pulling her arm away.

"I saw you earlier today," Hart said. "I guess you didn't see me."

"Oh?" Madison said. "No, I guess I didn't. I've been a little preoccupied today. Sorry."

Hart smiled. "So, what's up? Why are you preoccupied?"

"Yes," Madison said.

"Huh?" Hart said.

"I'm fine," Madison said.

Hart sighed. "Actually, what I asked you was—"

"Do you ever watch *Crime Time*?" Madison

blurted out. Sometimes, when she couldn't think of anything else, Madison would just say the first thing that came into her head. This was one of those occasions.

"You mean the TV show?" Hart asked.

Madison nodded.

Hart shrugged. "Sometimes I watch it. When there's nothing else on."

"Oh," Madison said. "There was a marathon over the weekend. I've seen every episode at least once."

But Hart didn't seem very interested in the fine points of *Crime Time*. In fact, he'd turned completely around and was staring in the opposite direction. Madison bit her lip. Was she boring him? She needed a better topic of conversation. Fast.

"What did *you* do this weekend?" Madison asked. But before Hart could answer, Poison Ivy appeared from around the corner.

Once upon a time, Ivy Daly had been Madison's best friend. But that had all changed in third grade. Now Ivy was her number-one enemy. To make matters worse, it seemed as though Ivy always appeared when Hart was around.

"Hiya, Hart," Ivy said, smiling sweetly. She turned to Madison and sneered.

"Hello, Ivy," Hart replied.

"So . . ." Ivy said in a singsong voice. She cocked her hip, waiting for Hart's next comment. "So?" she asked again.

But Hart didn't say anything else. He just stared.

"I like your sweater," Ivy told him. She batted her eyelashes.

Hart grunted a little. "Uh-huh."

"Do you like mine?" Ivy asked, looking down at her own lavender short-sleeved top.

Madison wanted to yell, *Who cares about your ugly sweater!* Instead, she gritted her teeth and bit her tongue. She couldn't lash out. Madison didn't want Hart to think she was being mean.

Ivy was still pushing for a compliment from Hart, but he wasn't offering any.

Madison decided to set a little trap for Ivy. She would work some reverse psychology on the enemy.

"Gee, Ivy," Madison crooned. "Your hair looks different. What did you do?"

Ivy fell for it. She tossed her hair and grinned. "It is a great haircut, isn't it? And my hair looks good with this outfit, doesn't it?" she said.

Hart snickered.

Ivy glared at him. "I'm sorry," she asked Hart. "Is something funny?"

His eyes opened wide. "Oh, no," he said, smiling and staring straight ahead.

Madison couldn't believe it. Usually Hart was the one who acted nicer than nice. But this time, he couldn't seem to keep a straight face. He had snickered! He had smiled! He was giving Ivy the total brush-off.

"Okay, well, that's okay. . . ." Ivy stammered. "Are you leaving school now? I'll walk out with you. . . ."

She reached for Hart's arm. Hart backed away.

"Actually, I was just talking to Madison here. . . ." Hart said.

Madison almost fainted when he said that. She watched Ivy squirm, nibbling on her lip, very confused. Was Poison Ivy going to start foaming at the mouth? Madison hoped so. It would have made a great picture.

"Well . . . ?" Ivy said. She'd run out of ideas.

"See you later," Hart said.

Ivy held her book bag to her chest and pouted, glaring in Madison's direction. "Later?" she said. "Sure. Whatever."

As she strutted away, Hart made a funny face. "Ivy is so weird sometimes, like she's queen of the school or something," he said, and paused. "But she doesn't have a clue."

Madison couldn't believe what she was hearing.

Hart's putting Ivy down was the next best thing to Hart's actually telling Madison that he liked her—almost.

He accompanied Madison to her locker. As she opened it, her flute case fell onto the floor, and he picked it up.

"I didn't know you played flute," Hart said.

Madison grabbed the case from him. "I don't play as much as I used to."

"You know, I play piano," Hart said.

"Really?" Madison said. She turned toward him. They were standing so close she could almost feel his breath.

"Maddie!" Aimee yelled from down the hall. Madison jumped as Aimee and Fiona raced up to her and slapped her on the back.

"Hi, Hart," Fiona said.

Hart looked flustered and stepped away from Madison. "Hey, Fiona. Hi, Aim."

"Hey, Hart, how's the puppy?" Aimee asked. When her dog Blossom had had puppies, Hart's parents had bought one of them for him. He'd named it Bones Jones.

"Bonesy ate the rug in my dad's study," Hart said.

Madison giggled. "Whoops," she said.

Hart laughed. "He's cute, though. How's Blossom doing?"

"Blossom is still recovering from having pups. She spends most of her time with the two babies we kept," Aimee said.

"What did you call them?" Hart asked.

"Yin and Yang!" Fiona interrupted. "Can you believe it? Aimee's mom is so New Age. Hey, has anyone seen Egg around? I wanted to talk to him before soccer practice."

"I think he went to the gym," Hart said.

"Yeah, he's Mr. Workout these days, isn't he?" Madison said sarcastically.

"Oh! I have to go, then," said Fiona, reaching into her own locker and stuffing her bag with books for homework. "I'll E you later," she called out to Madison and Aimee.

Madison waved. "E you later," she repeated, hoping that Aimee might disappear, too, and leave Madison alone with Hart once again.

But it was Hart who left next. He said his good-byes and headed down the hall to meet with a teacher.

"You and Hart make a cute couple," Aimee said when he was gone.

"Aimee!" Madison shouted. "You're embarrassing me. Quit it. We are not a couple. We're friends."

"Yeah, right!" Aimee said, making a face.

"Want to walk home together?" Madison asked.

"Can't," Aimee said. "Dance class."

"Bummer," Madison said.

Aimee leaned in and whispered. "So, what were you and the Hunk talking about?"

"The *what*?" Madison laughed.

"You look pretty today," Aimee said.

Madison blushed. "Oh, no, I don't. And we were talking about nothing, as usual. I get so tongue-tied when we're alone together. It's dumb."

Aimee shrugged. She slung her ballet bag over her shoulder. "So what? He still likes you. Even if you are *bor*ing!"

Madison whacked Aimee's arm. "I'm going to get you for that!" she cried as Aimee jogged down the corridor.

"Later!" Aimee cried.

Since no one was available to walk with her, Madison turned back to her locker, got her stuff, and headed out of school by herself. It was a warm afternoon, so she tied her thick red cardigan around her waist and walked along the sunny side of the street. The air smelled like autumn, a perfect mix of leaves, burning firewood, and damp mud. Trees that had worn full coats of red and gold only a few weeks earlier had shed them in piles along the road, and their branches were bare.

As soon as she arrived home, Madison headed upstairs to finish up the math homework from the night before—along with new math problems from that day's class. She curled up in the corner of her window seat, surrounded by her math book, her notebooks, and, of course, her laptop. She needed to finish typing the file she'd started before dinner started. But when Madison reached into her orange bag, she couldn't locate the disk she needed. She dumped the bag's entire contents onto the floor of her bedroom. Everything landed with a thud.

Madison looked frantically through the paper, books, and pencil shavings spread out on the floor.

There was no disk to be found.

"Maddie!" Mom called out. "Have you seen my keys?"

"No!" Madison called out. "I'll be right down."

When she came downstairs, Madison saw her mom looking around for the missing set of house and car keys.

"Where did you have the keys last?" Madison asked.

Mom frowned. "In the car. When I opened the door. I can't remember. I think I left them here on the hall table, but . . ."

"You never lose stuff," Madison commented.

"I know," Mom said. She shuffled through the pile of newspapers on a hall chair and then moved into the kitchen. "Maybe I left them on the counter?"

Madison and Mom both searched the kitchen from top to bottom. Madison looked under tables and chairs. Mom fished in the pockets of the coat she had been wearing.

Nothing.

"Rowrrooooooo!" Phin howled from the kitchen floor. He wanted them to pay attention to him, not the missing keys.

Madison threw Phin a chew bone to keep him quiet. He grabbed it between his teeth and trotted away. A few moments later, he returned. In his mouth was a fuzzy green slipper.

"Phin!" Mom yelled. "Were you in my room again?" she asked.

Phin dropped the slipper and trotted away.

When he came back a second time, he carried Madison's disk in his mouth.

"Phinnie!" Madison cried. "Where did you get that?"

Phin dropped the disk on the floor. His curlicue tail wagged very fast, as if he knew he had done something wrong.

Madison leaned over and retrieved the disk. She stuck it into the pocket of her jean shirt.

That's when she got her big idea.

"Mom!" Madison said. "I think I know where your keys are."

Taking the stairs two steps at a time, Madison raced up to Mom's bedroom. Phinnie followed her. She looked all around before she discovered the thing she was seeking—along with a whole bunch of other things.

There in Mom's closet, way in the back corner, was a small pile.

On the top of the pile were Mom's keys, right next to Mom's other green fuzzy slipper.

"Phinnie!" Madison said, laughing. "Look at this! You have Mom's keys, slipper, her scarf, two or three of those rawhide chew toys I thought you'd eaten already, your missing collar tags, a tennis ball . . . yuck!"

Madison recoiled. The tennis ball was wet with dog drool.

By now, Mom had joined them in the closet. "I had no idea our dog was such a little pack rat."

"Me, neither," Madison said.

"Rowrroroooooo!" Phin barked as if he knew what they were saying.

Madison handed Mom the missing keys. "Here you go," she said.

Mom shook her head with disbelief. "You saved the day, honey bear," Mom said, grinning.

"See?" Madison smiled. "I told you *Crime Time* was good for something."

Mom pocketed the keys. "Okay, okay. Finish up your homework, and then let's eat."

Madison gave Mom a kiss on the cheek and skipped into her bedroom. Phin followed close behind. Madison popped the recovered disk into her computer.

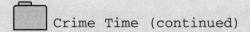 Crime Time (continued)

Rude Awakening: Snoop and ye shall find.
I don't want to make a big deal out of this, but I think I may have a knack for solving mysteries. I know locating a missing disk and keys isn't like finding some bank robber, but it's a start.
Move over, Major.
Madison DeMille is on the case.

Chapter 3

The following afternoon, Madison found herself back in the media lab. She decided to finish her homework before heading to her afternoon flute lesson with Mr. Olivetti. Try as she might, however, Madison's laptop distracted her. Instead of studying, she found herself surfing.

She opened her e-mailbox.

FROM	SUBJECT
✉ JeffFinn	Fwd: Fwd: Read This
✉ GoGramma	Miss You
✉ Boop-Dee-Doop	FALL FLING-A-DING
✉ Bigwheels	HELP!!!

Dad sent the first e-mail.

From: JeffFinn
To: MadFinn
Subject: Fwd: Fwd: Read This
Date: Tues 12 Oct 10:09 AM
Hey, Maddie,

Stephanie and I are looking forward
to dinner tonight. Steak and fries,
as requested--your favorite.

Have you heard this one? Why did
the skeleton cross the road? Because
the chicken dared him! She said the
skeleton had no guts!!!

Couldn't resist.

Love, Dad

P.S.: Call me when you get home from
school and I'll pick you up.

"Oh, Dad," Madison moaned to herself. "So
lame."

Dad was always sending her bad, *bad* jokes, especially around the holidays. She quickly hit DELETE and
moved on to the next e-mail.

25

From: GoGramma
To: MadFinn
Subject: Miss You
Date: Tues 12 Oct 12:11 PM

How are things in Far Hills, my
dear? Your mother has not written or
called in DAYS and I was a little
worried. I know how often you check
your mailbox online so this is the
best way to get in touch. I'm the
same. Still playing cards with Mabel
and knitting that afghan I promised
you for this winter. I found the
perfect sky-blue yarn.

Write back when you can! Love to my
favorite pug.

xoxoxo

Gramma

Madison made a mental note to tell Mom about
Gramma Helen's message. She knew the truth:
Gramma had probably called once, gotten a busy
signal, and then given up and imagined the worst.
She did that sometimes.

Another e-mail had a Fall Fling-a-Ding sale coupon
attached from Boop-Dee-Doop, Madison's favorite
online store. Perfect! Madison thought. She had just

been ogling a pair of cute corduroy pants with flowers embroidered near the cuff. She saved the e-mail
on her hard drive and clicked on the next message.

It was from her long-distance keypal, who sounded
worried.

From: Bigwheels
To: MadFinn
Subject: HELP!!
Date: Tues 12 Oct 1:58 PM

Where are you?!! I wrote you two
different e-mails from school
this AM and they came back to me
undeliverable. Are you having probs
w/ur bigfishbowl address? I know
sometimes mail comes back when the
server is too busy.

INYH. My parents are arguing again.
Only this time I think it's for
real. Is this the beginning of the
Big D for me? Even worse, my little
sister is throwing these huge
tantrums 18ly too (she is SOOOO
annoying. When she whines she sounds
like a sick Muppet). I feel like I'm
in the middle of this huge mess.
What a crummy place 2 be.

Please go online 18r so we can talk.

I'll be in our usual room CHTTRBX
tonite after 6 my time, ok? Can u do
it? Be there or B(2).

Yours till the Web sites,

Victoria aka Bigwheels

Madison knew she would probably be at Dad's after six, but she hoped she could find time to chat with Bigwheels anyway, maybe on Dad's computer. She hit SAVE to make sure she didn't forget the time or the name of the chat room.

"Shhhh! Someone will hear us!"

Madison turned abruptly from her laptop. Someone squealed somewhere among the stacks of books behind the place where Madison was sitting.

"I said, shut *up!*" another voice yelled.

The voice sounded familiar, but Madison wasn't sure whose it was.

She leaned to the side of her chair, craning her neck to get a view of whoever was talking. But now she couldn't make out any real words—just hushed tones and giggles. She got up slowly from her seat and slid behind a tall bookshelf. Nose to nose with a book of biography, Madison held her breath so she wouldn't make a sound. She could hear bits and pieces of conversation from where she stood.

"They're rare!" one girl said. She spoke in a deep whisper.

". . . Never find out," the other girl said. Her voice sounded more like the screaming wheels of a roller coaster.

Madison could make out a few other scraps of conversation in between: "bag," "music," and "Don't tell."

Who was there? What were they talking about?

Madison bit her tongue and peered through the books on the shelves. Could she identify the two speakers? For a brief moment, Madison thought it might be Poison Ivy and one of her drones, Joan or Rose, but she couldn't be sure. Her mind raced.

What am I doing here? Madison thought. I never eavesdrop. Why am I eavesdropping? Who's over there? Maybe I should just turn the corner and speak to them? What is the big secret? Maybe it's nothing. I'm being so nosy. What am I—?

Madison gulped.

She realized that the voices had stopped. All at once, she dropped to her knees and pretended to be reading a book on the bottom shelf, called *Astrophysics Made Easy.*

Like anyone would believe she was actually reading that.

"Hide it," the nonsqueaky voice whispered.

Madison's ears pricked up again.

"So-o-o-o-o-o much fun!" the other voice said.

Madison realized she could see who was talking through the books on the bottom shelf. She saw a pair of funny blue loafers next to a pair of ratty-looking tennis sneakers with pink shoelaces.

Whose shoes were those?

What would Major DeMille have done in a situation like this? Madison wondered. Her detective instincts clicked into action. She needed to identify the sneakers and then investigate. Madison stood up slowly, brushed off her pants and took a deep breath. She walked to one end of the tall bookshelf and quickly looped around the other side.

"Excuse me," Madison said as she turned.

"Yeah?" A boy in a gray sweatshirt stood there holding a giant encyclopedia. "What are you looking at?"

"Um," Madison felt herself flush. "I thought . . . you were . . ." she stammered. "I thought . . . I heard . . . girls. . . ."

"Geek," the boy grunted under his breath.

"Eighth grader," Madison mumbled back.

But she didn't have time to be offended. Turning on her heel, she glanced around the library. Where had the girls disappeared to?

She spotted a torn slip of paper on the floor of the library. Had the mystery girls dropped it?

The time and address of an appointment were written in scrawled handwriting with big loops on the *y* and *q*.

Friday at 4 @ 411 Marquette Street

Marquette Street! Madison knew that address. It was near her house on Blueberry Street. She looked closely at the piece of paper. There was an image there, too, that she couldn't make out. It looked like a photograph. Was it a picture of a tree? Or was it a picture of the top of someone's head?

Madison wandered back to her bag and laptop, still open in the carrel where she'd been sitting.

"All alone?" someone said.

Madison turned and saw Ivy standing there.

"Where's Hart?" Ivy asked.

"Huh?" Madison replied.

"Sure," Ivy snarled. "Play dumb. Look, I don't know what is going on with you and Hart Jones, but I think you had better just back off. Okay?"

Madison blinked. "What are you talking about?" she said.

"You know," Ivy said, pursing her lips as if she were about to spit. "You know."

"I don't know," Madison said. "Ivy, I don't know what you're—"

Ivy held up her hand to stop Madison from finishing her sentence. "Don't even bother," she said.

Ivy spun around and headed toward the other side of the library.

Madison collapsed onto the chair by her laptop, still clutching the sheet of paper she'd found on the floor.

What was going on around there?

Slowly, she pulled her belongings together and packed them neatly into her orange bag. It was three-thirty. She pulled her flute case out and laid it on top of everything else, and then she went downstairs to the music room.

Mr. Olivetti was late, as usual. Madison sat on a stool in the middle of the room, tapping the ground with her foot. She lifted her flute and began to play.

Screeeeeeeeeeeeeeeeeeeeeeeeeee!

Madison recoiled at her own playing. It was if she'd forgotten how. Her mind was on other things.

Marquette Street.

Madison thought again about the ratty sneakers and the squeaking voice. Where had she heard that voice before? It wasn't Ivy's.

Or was it?

"Miss-a-Finn!" Mr. Olivetti raced into the music room carrying an oversize briefcase. While most other male teachers wore plain ties and pants, and didn't wear jackets, Mr. Olivetti wore a bright red bow tie and a sharp-looking suit. He spoke in a thick Italian accent. "My-a-goodness," he said. "I'm-a-so late!"

"No prob," Madison mumbled.

"So, we are ready to make-a-some music, yes?" Mr. Olivetti asked.

Madison nodded. "Yes," she said.

"We have much to do, Miss-a-Finn," he said, patting her on the shoulder. "Let's-a-start with tone. Can you hold a middle B-natural?"

Madison smiled. She nodded. "I can try," she said, positioning the flute in front of her.

Screeeeeeeeeeeeeeeeeeeeeeeeee!

Mr. Olivetti made a face, as if he'd eaten a lemon.

"Ahhh," he said slowly. "After this-a-we practice scale work. Two octaves, yes?"

Madison nodded again. It was harder than hard to relearn a musical instrument. She wasn't sure if she really wanted to be there. Watching *Crime Time* and hanging out at home with Phinnie were a lot more fun.

After the lesson was over and Madison was certain she had no spit left (flute-playing always dried out her mouth), Madison headed for home. She stopped in the locker room first to see if maybe Fiona was there. Fiona usually finished up her soccer practice around four o'clock.

Fiona was not in the locker room when Madison arrived. Madison sat down on a bench and readjusted the books and laptop in her bag. She would be homeward bound after all.

Just as she got up to leave, however, she saw the sneakers—the ratty sneakers with the pink laces that she had seen in the library before. They were planted neatly under a bench directly facing Madison, next to a row of clogs, shoes, and more sneakers.

Madison looked around to see if the owner of the shoes was nearby. She listened close for a squeaky voice. But she heard nothing.

Until Poison Ivy showed up *again*.

"Oh, God. It's you," Ivy groaned.

She wore a sweatshirt and had pulled her hair back with a pink elastic band covered in butterflies; little butterfly barrettes were clipped to the side of her head. Madison guessed that Ivy had stayed at school for a dance or yoga workshop. Far Hills Junior High was trying to offer all sorts of new after-school programs. Ivy was always first in line to sign up for anything that sounded "cool." She always wanted to do anything that her favorite movie stars liked to do.

"Are you following me?" Ivy sneered.

"No. I was just waiting for someone," Madison said, wishing she could be invisible. She didn't feel like getting into it with Ivy for the second time that day.

Of course, the torture didn't stop there. A moment later, Ivy's drones, Rose and Joanie, came into the locker room wearing the latest terry-cloth sweatpants and faded-to-perfection T-shirts. The backside of Rose's pants read: *FOXY*. The backside of Joan's read: *PRETTY*. As if! Madison's mom would never have let her wear anything like *that*—especially to school.

"I just saw Hart," Ivy said with a grin to the group. "Outside. He stopped what he was doing just to talk to me. What do you think of *that*?"

"Goody for you," Madison said with a growl. She hoisted her bag onto her back. "Goody, goody, *goody*."

Ivy made a disgusted look. "Look who's talking, Miss Goody-goody. And you know what? I feel sorry for you," she said.

"You feel sorry for me?" Madison snapped. "Ha! I feel . . . I feel . . ."

Madison wanted to say something sharp . . . something smart . . . something that would knock Poison Ivy's perfect pink socks right off.

But her mind drew a blank. With Ivy and her drones all there, it was three against one, and the pressure was just too much. Madison skulked out the door of the locker room without saying another word.

Ivy and the drones laughed—or was it, squealed?— as Madison exited the locker room. As she headed for home, Madison considered the distinct possibility that maybe Ivy Daly's *was* the voice she'd heard in the library earlier in the day.

Maybe Ivy was up to no good—again?

She had to find out for sure.

Chapter 4

It was already twenty minutes since Madison had called, and Dad still hadn't come over to pick her up for dinner. Madison sat outside on the front porch with her laptop. She typed a message to Bigwheels as she waited.

```
From: MadFinn
To: Bigwheels
Subject: Re: HELP!!
Date: Tues 12 Oct 5:31 PM
Hey it's me. I'll try 2 chat tonite
but I'm going to my dad's for dinner
so I don't know 4 sure. Maybe we can
talk tomorrow night?

BTW: I'm sorry your parents are
fighting again. That's a big bummer.
```

There's nothing worse than listening to two grown-ups howling at each other. I wish I could give you this perfect advice, like, tell them they need to argue in "noise only" zones away from you--like in the car or in the basement behind the boiler.

When my mom and dad argued, I basically hid. That's my advice. TM--Don't get involved.

This isn't very good advice, I know. But I'm not feeling very smart about things today. I ran into my enemy Ivy at school twice and both times she shot me down. I never have a good comeback. In fact, you may just want to ignore EVERYTHING I say. Period.

I had a flute lesson today. I sounded like a cross between a high-pitched bird and a squeaky brake. I think my teacher actually covered his ears during my lesson. J/K but I do have some serious practicing to do.

Don't forget that Crime Time has a repeat of last week's episode coming up tomorrow. You do watch the show, right? You'd better!!! We can compare notes.

Yours till the music boxes,

Maddie

P.S.: I think I may have a few
mysteries of my own brewing in Far
Hills. I found this strange paper
in the library. ML.

In an instance of perfect timing (and perhaps an omen of better things to come), Madison saw Dad's car pull into the driveway just as she hit SEND.

Dad didn't even get out of the car. He just honked.

"Bye, Mom!" Madison yelled as she stuck her head back into the house and placed her laptop on the chair in the hall. "Love you!"

Mom called out from her office. "Love you, too!"

Madison leaned down and scratched the top of Phin's head. He was dancing around her legs, as if to say, "Don't go!"

But after a quick kiss to his furry little head, she went, anyway.

Madison scooted down the porch steps and got into the front seat of Dad's car.

"Hello, Miss Maddie," Dad said, smiling. "Don't you look fetching tonight! Is that a new ensemble?"

"Dad," Madison said. "You should be a fashion critic. You always notice what I wear."

Dad chuckled. "It's your stepmother's influence,"

he said. "She leaves those fashion magazines lying around the apartment."

Madison smiled. Dad had finally married his longtime girlfriend, Stephanie, and she *had* made a difference in his life, and not only by improving his fashion sense. Stephanie had made Dad laugh again.

"How's my dog?" Dad asked. Ever since the Big D, Madison had been convinced that Dad missed Phin as much as he missed her.

"He's really a pack rat!" Madison chimed in.

Dad looked confused. "Rat?"

"Mom and I caught him stealing stuff in the house and storing it in the back of her closet. You know, like a pack rat. He's been doing it for weeks."

"Phin? A thief?" Dad feigned shock.

"Oh, Dad," Madison sighed. "He is! He even stole a disk out of my orange bag and hid it."

"What else did he steal?" Dad asked.

Madison recounted the full list of missing items.

Dad grinned. "Clever pooch, isn't he? I think he went through a phase like this once or twice before. I seem to remember losing a pair of cuff links. . . ."

"Don't you think I was pretty clever, Dad, for figuring out what Phin was doing?" Madison asked.

Dad nodded. "Very, very clever."

"Cut it out, Dad!" Madison grinned and punched Dad in the shoulder. "I was thinking . . . maybe I should be a detective when I grow up," Madison said.

"A detective, huh?"

"Like on *Crime Time*," Madison said.

"What's that?"

Madison gasped. "Only the best show on television, Dad. When we get to your apartment we are totally going online, and I can show you their Web site."

As soon as they arrived at Dad's, Madison dragged Dad into his office and told him to boot up his computer. They opened the Web site for *Crime Time*. Major DeMille's face filled the screen of the monitor and then faded to black. A voice crackled over the computer speakers.

"*It's* Crime Time! *Do you have what it takes to solve critical crimes?*" the voice said. All at once, various images flew across the screen: fingerprints, police badges, the chalk outlines of bodies, and even spatterings of blood.

"Neat, huh?" Madison said, raising her eyebrows.

Dad chuckled. "Yes, it's cool," he said, clicking a few other buttons on the site. "But is this show violent?"

"No, no, no! That's why it's so much better than those other shows. It's all about the detective work." Madison leaned over his shoulder. "Press that, Dad."

Dad clicked on a magnifying-glass icon, and a text checklist appeared. They started reading the list together.

Do You Have What It Takes to Be a Crime Time Detective?

1. Eyes and ears OPEN. No snoozing on the job if you're serious about Crime Timing. Sharpen the senses by reading lots of books, asking questions, and listening closely.
2. Examine a crime scene with smarts. Look for things that seem out of place. Take mental pictures--and written notes.
3. Collect evidence carefully. That means no trespassing, no poking your nose where it's not allowed. Finders keepers only if it's out in the open.

"What are you two doing in here?" Stephanie asked as she walked into Dad's office. She had just come home from work.

Madison perked up. "How's your arm?" she asked.

"Ouch," Stephanie said with a smile. "Thank goodness it isn't the wrist of the hand I write with. Then I'd really be in trouble."

"Hey, Stephanie, have you ever watched *Crime Time*?" Madison asked.

She showed Stephanie the Web site and explained her newfound ambition.

"A detective!" Stephanie exclaimed. "That's what I wanted to be when I was your age!"

"Really?" Madison said, surprised.

Dad just smiled. "Why don't I leave you two to the detective chatter, and I'll go put the finishing touches on dinner?"

Stephanie collapsed onto the love seat in the corner of Dad's office and crossed her legs.

"So what started all this interest in *Crime Time*?" Stephanie asked Madison. "I've seen that show a few times. It's good."

Madison explained about how she was the show's number-one fan and how she had decided that maybe she could solve crimes, too. After all, she had solved Phinnie's doggy crime spree. Madison told her about the secret note and the sneakers with pink laces from the library.

"Sounds like you're onto something. . . ." Stephanie said.

"I think so!" Madison said.

"Believe it or not, Maddie," Stephanie explained, "sometimes my friends used to call me Sleuthie instead of Stephie at my high school back in Texas."

"No way!" Madison said. "That's so cool! You solved crimes for real?"

"Well . . ." Stephanie made a funny face. "Sorta. I didn't catch any big-time criminals or anything. It was strictly small stuff."

Stephanie told Madison a long story about chasing clues around to find out who was painting graffiti on lockers at her Bellville, Texas, high school. After she had located empty paint cans, spotted kids lurking by their lockers late in the day, and noted various suspicious activity, Stephanie prepared to go directly to the principal with the evidence. No one believed her at first, so she poked around some more.

"That sounds cool," Madison said. "What did you find out?"

"I found out that you have to be careful when you start detective work," Stephanie said. "You may not always understand what you find."

"What do you mean?" Madison asked.

"Sometimes, when you start snooping, you can't stop. And you may end up jumping to conclusions, or suspecting people who haven't done anything wrong. It can get messy. I lost one of my close friends that way."

"Why? Was she the graffiti artist, or what?"

Stephanie shook her head. "No, it was a boy— and he wasn't the artist, but I thought he had paint on his coat, and I suspected him. Our friendship was never the same again."

"Wow," Madison said. "I never thought about it that way. But you know what? Now I know not to snoop where I'm not wanted. I won't make that mistake. Besides, it's not like I'm trying to be a *real* detective. I'm not on *Crime Time* or anything. This is just some silly thing from school. . . ."

"I know," Stephanie nodded. She jumped up from the sofa. "You'll make a super school detective," she said, rubbing Madison's back. "Hey, let's go eat."

They wandered into the dining room.

Dad's steak and fries were waiting.

When she arrived back home, Madison was tired—and she still had math homework to do. She went to her room and powered up her laptop. Phinnie curled up at her feet.

Of course, fifteen minutes into a set of problems, Madison's mind wasn't on numbers at all. She was in her files, clicking, deleting, and organizing. She could finish her math work later—like the next day, in a free period before class.

Madison scrolled through some of the alphabetized files, her head spinning. In addition to about a hundred files marked *Boys* and *Hart*—clearly her favorite subjects—Madison had files on almost every other topic imaginable.

```
Bad News
Class Notes
The Conspiracy
The Dance
Only the Lonely
Rain
Surprises
What I Don't Know
```

Madison laughed at the sight of her extensive files. Reading through the topics like that made her life seem way more interesting than it actually was—at least, more interesting than usual.

Madison clicked NEW. She wanted to create a new set of files for her detective work. After all, a super sleuth couldn't work without information at her fingertips. Project number one would be to scan the mysterious scrap of paper Madison had located in the library. Later she could also scan a street map showing the exact location of 411 Marquette Street.

Madison dug the note out of her bag and placed it onto the scanner. While she was waiting for the machine to make the scan, a light blinked in the corner of the screen.

Who would have sent e-mail so late in the day? Was Bigwheels in trouble again?

```
From: Dantheman
To: MadFinn
Subject: The Clinic Needs U
Date: Tues 12 Oct 7:13 PM
Yo, Maddie whassup. I'm here w/my mom
@ the clinic. Where have u been we
miss u. Ok. We really really could use
ur help here tomorrow b/c there are
like 100 new animals. Ok not a 100
but close. N e way, can u come after
school w/me and help out? We need
```

someone who knows the ropes and ur the best. Lemme know.

Bye,

Dan

Madison wrote back immediately. Dantheman was Dan Ginsburg, one of her guy friends at FHJH—and her best friend at the Far Hills Animal Clinic. Together with Dan, Madison volunteered to clean cages, cuddle scared pets that were up for adoption, and even help the clinic's Dr. Wing prepare for certain veterinary procedures. Once she had assisted when a sick ferret came in for emergency paw surgery.

Dan didn't even have to ask if Madison would volunteer. Of course she would! It didn't matter that Madison was backlogged with homework, flute lessons, and now, her detective work. Madison loved animals very much—maybe even more than *Crime Time*, if that were possible.

But if Madison was going to do everything she wanted to do tomorrow, she needed her sleep. She shut down the computer and leaned over Phin.

"Phinnie . . ." Madison whispered.

"Rrrrrrrrrrrrrrrrrrrr," Phin snored.

Madison kissed the top of his head. "Good night, my doggy prince," she whispered in his ear before turning out the light.

Chapter 5

"Maddie!" Dan called out to Madison in the crowded hallway at school on Wednesday afternoon. *"Maddie!"*

Madison nearly crashed into a pack of ninth graders when she heard him.

"Wait!" Dan yelled again. He was gasping for air by the time he finally caught up to Madison.

"Dan," Madison said. "This is so funny. I was just looking for you."

"I've been looking for you all day," Dan replied. "I saw you before my science class, but you were outside the music room talking to Mrs. Montefiore, and then later before English, but you were going into Gibbons's room, and I was going in the other direction. . . ."

"That's weird. I didn't see you either place," Madison said.

"What do I have to do to get your attention, set off flares?" Dan quipped.

He and Madison laughed. Unfortunately, their laughter drew the unwanted attention of the same pack of ninth graders Madison had met earlier.

"What's your problem? Is something funny?" one of the boys in the group growled at Dan.

"Yeah, what are you laughing at, fat boy?" another one snapped.

Dan gulped. Usually if he got picked on by kids at school, it was for his weight. In fifth grade, Dan's nickname had been Pork-O. But there was a big difference between a good friend's making up a nickname for him—and a bully's doing it.

"Um . . . um . . ." Dan stammered. He could feel the sweat on his neck.

"Let's split," another kid in the pack said. "Time to leave the losers alone to do whatever it is loser seventh graders do. . . ."

Madison felt her fists clench.

If she were only a little taller . . . and a little stronger . . .

Luckily, the ninth-grade boys got bored fast. They were on to the next "loser" down the hall. They walked on, chuckling to themselves.

"That was close," Madison said. "Those guys gave you beady-eyed little stares like they were sharks. . . ."

"And I was the raw meat," Dan said with a snort. Madison giggled.

"So, are you coming to the clinic?" Dan asked.

"Huh? You didn't get my e-mail?" Madison asked.

Dan shook his head. "No, but my e-mail was down last night," he explained. "What did it say?"

"Of course I'm coming to the clinic," Madison said. "How could I miss it? You made it sound like such an emergency. A hundred new animals? Hey, if you need help, I'm your helper."

"Aces," Dan said. "My mom is working this afternoon, too. She always says you're the best volunteer. Well, next to me, that is."

Dan's mom, Eileen, was a nurse at the clinic. She was in charge of all of the business of Dr. Wing, the primary veterinarian.

Madison and Dan stopped at their lockers, waved good-bye to a few friends who passed them in the hallway, and made their way out the lobby door. They would have to ride the bus over to the clinic. Madison searched her pockets for quarters. Dan lent her one, and they boarded the bus.

When they arrived at the clinic, it didn't seem as busy as Madison had expected. There was only one man in the waiting room, with a cat carrier. Piped-in music played a chorus of "Monster Mash," in honor of the upcoming Halloween holiday.

"Madison!" Eileen cried, when she saw the kids come inside. "What a surprise!"

"Surprise?" Madison eyed Dan suspiciously. "What do you mean? Dan told me you have a lot of new animals and that you needed help. . . ."

"Oh, sure, we always need help," Eileen said with a wink. "I think today we have two new kittens in the back just waiting for you."

"Two?" Madison echoed.

As Eileen walked away, Madison turned and shot a look at Dan.

"What's going on around here, Dan? Where are the hundred new animals, Dan? Huh? Huh?"

She nudged him hard with her elbow. He grabbed Madison's arm and pulled her into the back area, where the animal cages were kept. Dan kept looking around as if he were afraid someone might hear them.

"Would you mind, please, telling me what is going on around here?" Madison asked.

"Look," Dan whispered. "The reason I made up that stuff about lots of new animals was because I needed a way—any way—to get you in here."

"Get me in here? What are you talking about?" Madison asked. "All you had to do was ask. You didn't need to lie."

Dan glanced around again. His voice got very low. "Well, this really *is* an emergency. Sort of. My mom doesn't know about it yet. I've been covering it up."

"Covering *what* up?" Madison asked, confused. "Dan, what are you talking about?"

Dan explained that some supplies were missing from the back cabinet. The stash of chew toys had been picked over and some taken. And someone was taking the kittens out of their cages when they weren't supposed to. Since Dan was in charge of the back area, he feared getting in trouble with his mom and Dr. Wing; just last month they'd gotten upset when another volunteer had left a parrot cage open. There had been bird poop everywhere.

"Dan, you're being ridiculous," Madison said. "No one will get mad at you because someone else took stuff."

"You don't get it," Dan said very seriously. "Mom told me that if we lose stuff or if animals get loose, she'll make me work in the office instead of back here. I can't do that, Maddie. So I have to find out who's really messing around and put a stop to it fast."

Madison paused thoughtfully. "Gee, maybe that is a problem. Do you have any leads?" She almost sounded like a real detective.

"Leads? Well," Dan sighed. "Did you ever see anything unusual around here when you were volunteering?"

"Not really," Madison shook her head. "Unless you count the guy who brought in that two-headed snake that time."

"Remember that? Whoa. That was definitely unusual," Dan said.

"I've never seen any strange behavior from volunteers, if that's what you mean," Madison added. She thought about the missing disk, the note in the library, and then said, "Maybe I can help."

Dan smiled. "I was hoping you'd say that. You're always good with this kind of stuff."

"Really?" Madison asked.

"Yeah. You always talk about mysteries," Dan said.

While Dan mopped the floor in front of the cages, Madison organized the medicine cabinet. She carefully observed the three other volunteers who were at the clinic.

Hmmm. Was anyone acting suspicious?

One volunteer, Josie, was a visiting nurse who helped care for sick animals. Madison didn't think she was a suspect. She didn't look particularly interested in chew toys. Besides, she was a grandmother. Madison couldn't imagine someone who looked like Gramma Helen stealing, or even borrowing, sweet and furry little kittens.

Another volunteer seemed innocent for other reasons. Madison recognized Lana Waldorf as a student from FHJH. She'd seen Lana in the halls. Although Lana always acted a little strangely, Madison was sure she couldn't have been the thief. Lana had no reason to go into the back near the animals. She was only there to help Eileen with filing.

It was a third volunteer, named Rocky, who seemed to Madison like the guilty party. Rocky lingered by the kitten cages and then passed out chew toys to a pair of barking pups as Madison watched. He went back to the kittens and seemed awfully interested in one that was mewing loudly. And since Rocky was always coming and going, he was the only one who could have had the real time and opportunity to commit the clinic crimes.

Madison shared her conspiracy theory with Dan.

"I think Rocky's your man," Madison said in her best Nancy Drew voice.

"You think?" Dan mulled over the theory. "But Rocky's such a nice guy, Maddie. He's been volunteering here longer than me."

Well, Madison said to herself. Maybe the thief is a volunteer who didn't come back . . . or maybe it's someone who . . .

"Uh, excuse me?"

Out of nowhere, Lana strolled right up to Madison and Dan with a stack of files in her hand.

"Your mom is busy with someone up front, Dan. And I have a question. I'm sorry to bug you, but can you help me find some—"

"Lana!" Madison blurted out. "It's you!"

Lana nearly dropped all of the files on the floor when Madison said that.

Dan raised an eyebrow. "What did you say, Maddie?"

"Yeah, what did you say?" Lana repeated.

Madison put her hands on her hips. "Lana, have you been spending time by the kitten cages?" she asked matter-of-factly.

Lana turned ashen. "Huh?" she said, acting dumb. "No . . . I never . . . I don't know . . . what do you . . . um . . ."

She looked as if she were about to burst into tears.

A light went on in Dan's head. "Lana?"

"No, no, no!" Lana insisted. "I didn't steal . . . I just borrowed . . . I mean, I only took the kittens out because they were so cute. . . ."

"But you were just helping my mom with filing," Dan said. "You weren't supposed to come back here."

"I didn't think anyone would notice," Lana said. "Is it really wrong to hold the cats? They were purring. . . ."

"What about the dog treats?" Dan asked.

Lana turned even paler. "Oh," she said.

"You took those, too?" Madison asked.

Lana hung her head. "Yes. But I just wanted to give the dogs something extra. . . ."

"Well, you broke the rules," Dan said, shaking his head. "If my mom knew the cats had gotten out or that you used extra dog treats, I would have gotten into so much trouble. She's like a hawk about inventory. You know that."

Lana shrugged. "I guess. I'm sorry, Dan."

"Well, I have to tell my mom," Dan said. He went up front to get Eileen.

As Dan walked away, Lana turned to Madison with a puzzled look.

"How did you know it was me who did all that stuff?" she asked.

"There." Madison pointed to Lana's sweater. "Cat hair," she said.

"Oh, no," Lana sighed. "I didn't even think about that."

"Why didn't you just ask to work back here? Why did you sneak around?" Madison asked.

"I don't know. . . ." Lana said. "I wish I hadn't. Now I'll probably be asked to leave."

Fortunately for Lana, Eileen had no intention of asking Lana to go anywhere. As soon as she came into the back room with Dan, Eileen took Lana aside and told her that the clinic would give her a second chance. Lana promised she wouldn't go to the back or handle any of the animals anymore without permission.

Dan was mad. He didn't understand why his mom would let someone who was a sneak and a liar stay on as a volunteer at the clinic, especially when Eileen was always so hard on him.

But Madison understood. What Lana had done

wasn't really so bad. No kittens had been injured or stolen. The missing dog chews had gone to dogs already in the clinic. Where was the harm in that? Madison realized that part of figuring out any crime meant understanding the criminal, no matter how big or small. And in that moment, she understood Lana.

A bell rang out in the back room. It was the cuckoo clock by the water cooler.

"Five o'clock!" Madison said. She needed to call her mom to come and pick her up. Eileen told Madison she could use the phone on her desk.

"You know, Maddie, I was thinking. . . ." Dan said. "You're like that detective guy on television."

"You mean, Major DeMille? On *Crime Time*?" Madison asked, thrilled at hearing him make the comparison.

Dan nodded. "I was so clueless about who was messing with the kittens, but you figured it out just like *that*. I'm impressed."

Madison blushed a little. "Well . . . maybe I do have a knack for solving crimes. . . ." she said dreamily. "You think?"

A car honked outside. Madison's mom was there. Madison waved good-bye to Dan, Eileen, Lana, and the rest of the volunteers. She even stopped to pet an iguana in the front room.

Mission accomplished. She'd solved her second crime.

On the way back to their house, Mom stopped off at China Grill for some takeout dinner. As they picked up the food, Madison asked the person behind the register for extra duck sauce and fortune cookies, hoping for an extra-special fortune. After all, that could have made the difference between a good day and a bad day, in Madison's superstitious mind.

Mom headed for her office after their dinner of shrimp fried rice with broccoli. A very full Madison said good night and headed upstairs with Phin to her room. She needed to finish her homework and get ready for bed.

After reading one chapter in her American history book, Madison stopped working on her homework. As usual, she was far too tempted by the call of the Internet.

She went online.

Surprise! There was an e-mail from Bigwheels.

```
From: Bigwheels
To: MadFinn
Subject: Crime Time all the time
Date: Wed 13 Oct 4:12 PM
Sorry u couldn't chat yesterday but
we'll do it soon 4 sure.

I am addicted to that Crime Time TV
show now Maddie. U were soooo right.
It is soooo good. I especially like
```

that guy Major. Cute! Actually I'm
not bragging or n e thing but I
think that my friend Reggie looks a
little like him only younger. (I told
u that Reggie and I are talking
again right? He asked me to go with
him to the fall dance at my school.
I was so excited.)

I wrote you a poem last night
after I got ur e-mail. It's
about friendship. Do you like it?
J/W

Write back soon and tell me.

Yours till the bubble baths,

Vicki aka Bigwheels

Madison clicked onto the attachment at the end
of Bigwheels's e-mail and a document opened. It was
the poem.

For Madison

Sometimes friends are like flowers.
Petals open up and they hug you.
Colors are bright and warm
And if I'm feeling low
I can always count on a friend to know.
Friends say the right things at the right time.

They are smarter than smart.
Most of all, friends have heart.

Love,

Vicki

Bigwheels had written poems before, but this was the best one yet. Madison wished she could write a poem right back. What would she write about? Being a detective?

Madison clicked SAVE so she could keep the poem in a safe place in her files. Later she would print it out and stick it on the bulletin board in her room or maybe even put it inside her school locker.

Then Madison hit REPLY.

From: MadFinn
To: Bigwheels
Subject: Re: Crime Time all the time
Date: Wed 13 Oct 7:06 PM
UR2N2ME!!! Is it possible to be such good friends with someone I have never met? You proved that it is. I will love your poem forever and ever. Thanks. Thanks. Thanks.

I had to write back tonight because something BIG happened today. I went to the animal clinic and--drumroll,

please--I solved another mystery. For
real! It was only figuring out that
this girl was sneaking the kittens
out to play but no one else could
figure out who was doing it and I
don't want to sound full of myself
or anything but I DID.

Know what? I am having major (as in
MAJOR DeMille) karma about all this
snooping stuff. I can really do it.
Plus, this was my fortune cookie with
tonight's takeout dinner: YOU NEVER
HESITATE TO SOLVE THE MOST DIFFICULT
PROBLEMS. Get that? SOLVE, like
crimes, right? Isn't that just
perfect!?

Did u ever read Nancy Drew? I read
all those books in fourth grade but
I think I'm going to go back and
read them all again. I bet I could
learn a thing or 2 from her, doncha
think? Maybe I'll be the NEW Nancy
Drew. Detective Madison Finn at your
service. LOL.

Yours till Crime Time,

Maddie

P.S.: I really will write a poem 4 u
2 someday I hope!

As she hit SEND, Madison's mind swirled. What if she really *could* become the next super girl detective? What if Madison Francesca Finn became the youngest girl ever featured on the cover of *Time* magazine, with the headline *You Go Girl: Solving Crimes After School*? What if she got so big that she was actually invited to appear on *Crime Time*?

She caught her breath.

A guest spot on *Crime Time*! That could mean she would meet Major DeMille, for real. What could be better than that? Aimee and Fiona would be so jealous. . . .

"*Maddie!* Is your light still on? It's getting late!"

The sound of Mom's voice interrupted her thoughts. Madison jumped up from her bed and ran over to the door.

"Okay, Mom. I hear you! And I'm getting ready for bed!" Madison yelled back. She closed her laptop and headed into the bathroom.

After all, the sooner she brushed her teeth . . .

And the sooner she climbed into bed . . .

The sooner she would be back in the amazing dream starring Major DeMille!

Deep sleep couldn't come soon enough.

Chapter 6

"Dan, shut up!" Madison said at the lunch table at school on Thursday.

"Why? It's true," Dan said. "You *are* a real detective."

Egg cracked up. "How can you solve crimes, Maddie? You're scared of bugs!"

"What does *that* have to do with anything?" Aimee said.

Madison buried her face in her hands. Dan had told everyone about the cat caper at the clinic, including Hart, who was staring at her right at that moment.

"I think it's cool," Hart said to Madison. "Not everyone can figure out things like that. Dan couldn't."

"No kidding," Dan said.

"Hey, is that the girl who took the kittens?" Chet, Fiona's twin, asked, way too loudly. He pointed across the cafeteria to Lana, who just happened to be having lunch at the same time.

"Shhh!" Fiona shushed her twin brother. "I wish you didn't have such an open manhole for a mouth!"

Madison felt uncomfortable. She waved, so that Lana wouldn't worry that they were gossiping about her—even though they were.

"Lana Waldorf's in math class with me," Hart said. "I feel bad for her. She never gets any problems right."

"Some kids call her Lana Waldorfus," Egg said.

"What does *that* have to do with anything?" Aimee said again. "How about your nickname? After all, we call you 'Egg'!"

Drew snorted.

Everyone else at the table laughed, too.

"Egg is a really uncool nickname, isn't it?" Chet chimed in, laughing louder than everyone else.

"Shut it," Egg said.

That only made Chet laugh *louder*.

Egg leaned over and whacked Chet in the head with a notebook—hard.

Chet whacked back.

Then Egg punched Chet in the arm.

"Hey, guys, want to chill out? The cafeteria monitor is looking this way," Dan cautioned.

"Yeah, stop, or we'll *all* get Detention," Madison said.

"You guys started it," Egg moaned. "Making fun of my name is totally unfair."

Madison saw Fiona smile at Egg.

"I don't think Egg is a weird name," Fiona whispered. She always tried to make Egg feel better when things were looking bad. Of course, her sweeter-than-sweet attention only made Egg feel more embarrassed than ever. He stood up and moved down to the other end of the table.

The other guys followed his lead, moving to the side. They formed teams for spitball hockey, while the girls finished eating lunch.

Fiona tried not to look hurt when Egg edged away.

"Maddie," Aimee said, changing the subject a little. "I know you're way into this whole *Crime Time* mystery-puzzle thing. And I think it's cool that you helped Dan at the clinic. But I really don't see how it makes you a real live detective. . . ."

Madison took a sip of her chocolate milk. "You don't?" she said, sounding disappointed. Aimee's opinion mattered a lot to Madison.

"She's not a detective, she's a super snooper!" Fiona said, trying to sound cheery even though she was still sad about Egg.

"If you ask me, all this snooping around seems dumb," Aimee added. "It sounds like a waste of time."

Madison sighed. "You really think so? I like it."

"Why is it a waste of time if she likes doing it?" Fiona asked.

Aimee shrugged.

"No. Maybe you're right, Aim," Madison thought aloud.

Aimee shrugged again. "I don't know. I just think you're getting . . . a little obsessed."

Was she? Madison remembered the slip of paper she'd found in the library with the mystery address on it . . . and how she had been thinking about maybe stopping off at that address just to see what was happening . . . and how she thought maybe she'd uncover a strange and mysterious crime ring. . . .

Wait! That wasn't obsessed. Was it?

It didn't matter. Madison realized that she couldn't stop being a detective now. No matter what Aimee said, there were mysteries to solve. *Real* mysteries, right there at FHJH. And Madison was on the case.

"Hey!" Egg popped back over to the girls' side of the table. Fiona looked encouraged. "What are you three doing next week?" he asked.

"Um . . . coming to school," Aimee said matter-of-factly. "What are you doing? Going to Disney World?"

"Duh," Egg said. "I meant, what are you doing next Wednesday, when we have the day off?"

Madison had almost forgotten about the day that they were going to get because of testing and some faculty conference. Being off from school in the middle of the week was like playing hooky, only legally.

"Well," Egg said dramatically. By now the other guys had come back to the end of the table to sit with the girls. "Drew's mom offered to take all of us to the movies."

"*Mooo-vieeees!*" Hart chanted.

The other guys let out a roar and gave Drew high fives.

"Whoa! That is so nice, Drew!" Fiona gushed.

Drew smiled. "My mom says we can go see *Curse of the Diamond*, that new thriller that's playing over at the multiplex."

"Oh, I really, really want to see that one!" Madison shrieked. It was part thriller, part adventure, part mystery. In other words, it was Madison's favorite kind of flick.

"Me, too," Chet said. "I like mysteries."

"I think mysteries are dumb," Aimee said.

Madison stuck out her tongue. "Hey!"

"*Curse of the Diamond* got five stars on Movie Picks," Dan said. He was always up to date on what was hot and what was not, based on what he read online.

"Exactly who's going?" Hart asked as he walked up to the table.

"Let's see," Egg thought aloud, counting names on his fingers as he spoke. "There's Drew, me, Dan,

Hart, Chet, Fiona, Maddie, Aim, and Drew's friend Elaine, so far."

Madison felt a sharp pain in the middle of her chest. Drew was inviting Elaine?

Oh, no, Madison sighed to herself.

That meant the movie day would be a couples thing. Even though they were all traveling in a group, they were pairing off.

Madison glanced back over at Hart, who was working on a pudding snack. A little bit of chocolate had gotten on his chin, Madison noticed. But it made him look even cuter. How was that possible?

Ever since Madison and Hart had sort of admitted that they sort of liked each other, things had been sort of confusing when it came to group activities. A while back, Hart had suggested that he and Madison go *together* when the group went to the movies. But then they never went. And he had never asked again.

Drew and Elaine were boyfriend and girlfriend. Everyone knew that.

Fiona and Egg would definitely stay a couple. That was obvious.

Chet and Dan would probably pal around together, too, like an anticouple, but paired off nonetheless.

But what would Madison do? This was Hart's chance to make good on his original offer. For the very first time, maybe they would be declared a couple, too.

And if Hart didn't ask? At least Madison could hang with Aimee.

"Too bad I can't go," Aimee said all of a sudden, as if she'd been reading Madison's mind.

Madison shot a look back at her BFF. "Huh?" she asked, surprised. "Can't go?"

"Because I'll probably take some extra dance classes that day," Aimee said.

"Classes? What? Aim!" Madison cried. "Why? It's our day off from school and classes! Besides, don't you think you're doing a lot of dance? In fact, I think maybe you're becoming a little . . . obsessed. . . ."

Madison laughed at her own joke.

Aimee laughed, too. "I guess I deserved that."

Madison threw her arm around Aimee, "Can't you blow off dance class for once? This is going to be fun."

"I don't think so. . . ." Aimee stammered. "I don't want to see that movie, anyhow. I told you."

Madison backed off. Aimee was acting so weird. How could she not want to go on a group outing with her closest friends?

"So, everyone is cool with *Curse of the Diamond*?" Drew asked the people at the table.

Everybody nodded.

And so the plan was made.

When the lunch period officially ended, a few moments later, everyone went off to classes. Fiona and Aimee left together. Madison found herself walking out of the cafeteria alone. But then Hart came up and tapped her on the shoulder.

"Hey, Finnster," he said with a smile.

Madison swallowed a few deep gulps of air. This was it.

"Can you help me out? I have to work on some science work sheets from Mr. Danehy's class, but I have hockey practice. . . ."

Madison did a double take.

Hockey?

"We have such a good team this year. Egg and I think the Rangers have a shot at the division championships," Hart said. "And we have a really big match this weekend against Dunn Manor."

Madison tried to read between the lines. Was there a movie invitation hidden there somewhere? Was she missing something?

"You know, the coach says I can play right wing this season," Hart said, as if that could have made any sense to Madison.

"Ever watch *Crime Time*?" she asked, out of the blue, desperate to change the subject.

It didn't matter that Madison had already asked Hart about the show. Hart didn't even hear her question. He was talking slap shots, not crime scenes.

Maybe Hart didn't want to go to the movies with Madison. Maybe he didn't like her anymore. Maybe in the last twenty-four hours he'd gone back to liking Poison Ivy Daly.

The class bell rang.

"See you later, Finnster!" Hart said as he made a left turn, heading for his next class.

"Um . . . Hart . . ." Madison called out after him.

Hart turned and smiled. "Yeah?"

"You have pudding on your face," Madison said. As much as she liked him, Madison couldn't help herself.

As Hart stood there, struck speechless, Madison started off in the opposite direction, toward Mr. Gibbons's English class.

Madison fought her way through the throngs of kids in the hall. She pushed the heavy stairwell door and went up to the next floor, where there was a traffic jam of sorts on the steps. As the rest of the kids slowly shuffled up to the third floor, Madison felt her heart aching a little.

Then she heard something. It was squeaky, and very familiar.

Was it the voice from the library?

Madison's heart started to pound. Where was the voice coming from? She tried to squeeze in between two guys in front of her. But they weren't moving fast enough.

And the squeaky voice was receding.

As she reached the top landing and the crowd dispersed a little, Madison scrambled to see if she could locate the source of the voice.

But whoever it was who had been speaking had

vanished. And there was no time to look anywhere else.

The second class bell was about to ring.

Madison gasped and leaned against the wall. She was beginning to feel as if the person she had heard in the library the day before had been merely a figment of her imagination.

But that didn't matter. Madison knew that Major DeMille would never have given up when tracking a suspect. And so, she wouldn't, either.

Chapter 7

 Crime Time

Okay. Everything I loved about Hart
and his beautiful brown hair (yes it IS
beautiful and soft looking, and I can't
help staring at it) and his cool new
sneakers and his brains and the way he
talks and calls me Finnster and the way he
doesn't seem ever to mind when I embarrass
myself--all that means nothing right now.
Hockey stinks. Boys stink. Right now Hart
and the rest of the world seem like a HUGE
mystery to me.

And what's with Aimee? After the whole
lunchroom thing, I sat with her in Mr.

Gibbons's English class and she was blowing
off all my questions. She was blowing ME
off. I asked why she wouldn't go to Drew's
and she said she had dance class AGAIN.
Then she said that detective movies like
Curse of the Diamond are dumb. That really
bugs me. I don't go around saying how much
I hate things SHE likes. Do I?

Rude Awakening: Sometimes I feel like my
friendship has sailed--and I'm left behind,
sinking.

Madison quickly hit SAVE when she saw Fiona,
Aimee, and Lindsay walking down the hall toward
her. She clicked her orange laptop shut and jumped
up from where she'd been sitting on the hall floor.
The halls at FHJH were filling fast with kids from all
three grades.

"There you are!" Fiona cried. "I thought we were
all walking to school together this morning. It's
Friday! Where were you?"

"Oh, no," Madison said. "I forgot."

"That's because you're not thinking of your
friends anymore. All you think about is mysteries,"
Aimee said with a smirk.

Madison stuck out her tongue. "That's *so* not
true, Aim."

She turned to Fiona. "I'm sorry I spaced about the
morning walk. I feel like such a lame-o," Madison
said.

73

"Oh, whatever," Fiona said with a wide smile, quickly accepting the apology.

"Speaking of mysteries . . ." Lindsay started to say. No one was really listening at first, but then she said, "I heard there's a school mystery going on and it's already under investigation."

Madison pricked up her ears when she heard the words *mystery* and *investigation*, but she tried to play it cool in front of Aimee. She wasn't in the mood for another lecture on being obsessed—and she definitely was not in the mood to reveal anything to her friends about the scrap of paper from the library.

"How do you know so much?" Aimee asked.

Lindsay's voice got low. "I have connections," she said with a wink—and then she laughed. "The truth is, I was eavesdropping just outside the teachers' lounge."

Fiona covered her mouth. "I can't believe you did that!" she squealed.

"I can," Madison said with a giggle. "You were a spy in a former life, Lindsay, I swear."

"Anyway, I heard someone say that some precious object had been stolen," Lindsay continued. "Whatever that means . . ."

"Which teacher said that? Do you know?" Madison asked.

"I think it was one of the language teachers . . . or maybe Mr. Olivetti," Lindsay replied. "He had an accent."

"Mr. Olivetti!" Madison exclaimed. "My flute teacher?"

"What does 'precious object' mean?" Aimee scoffed. "Sounds like a bunch of hooey."

"A bunch of *what*?" Fiona said.

They all started to laugh.

"Hooey," Aimee repeated, trying hard herself not to laugh. "Hooey! I don't know. My dad says that all the time. It's a cool word."

"It sounds like something my gramps would say," Fiona said.

"Anyway," Lindsay continued, "the teachers sounded really worried, like there was a thief in the building. Everyone sounded scared that their classroom might be next. And they think the thief could be a student, or a couple of students, working together."

"Wow, that sounds serious," Fiona said.

"Come on," Aimee said. "Don't you think if there was a major theft in the building that we'd hear about it?"

"Maybe," Madison said. "But maybe not. The teachers could want to keep the problem under wraps so they can trap the criminal. . . ."

"The *criminal*?" Aimee interrupted. "Maddie, you sound like one of those mystery shows you watch."

"So?" Madison asked. "This is a mystery, isn't it?"

"Maybe you can solve it," Fiona said.

"Yeah, the teachers should come to you for help," Lindsay added.

Aimee rolled her eyes. Madison saw it.

"You don't think I can figure this out, do you?" Madison said to Aimee directly.

Aimee shook her head. "Whatever. Do whatever you want."

"Why are you so negative all the time lately?" Madison asked. "It's really beginning to bug me."

Fiona and Lindsay backed off a little. At first they'd been joking, but now Madison and Aimee were staring each other down.

"I just think you'd better be careful, Maddie," Aimee said. "All this mystery stuff has you sticking your nose into everyone's business and asking too many questions."

"Too many?" Madison said. "What, is there a limit on questions or something?"

"I just think you should watch your back," Aimee said.

"Wow, Aim," Lindsay said. "Don't you think you're being a little hard on Maddie?"

"Why does she have to watch her back?" Fiona asked. "Is someone following her or something?"

Madison crossed her arms. "You're just mad," she blurted out, "because I might get noticed for this and I have a guy who likes me and . . ."

She stopped in midsentence.

Aimee looked down at the ground.

Madison felt a knot in her chest. She wanted to take back what she had said. She *needed* to take it back.

Fiona and Lindsay stood there, not saying anything.

Kids rushed all around the four of them as they stood there, dumbfounded.

"I have to go to class," Aimee finally said. She reached into her book bag and pulled out a tube of lip gloss, carefully applying some to her lips.

"Aim," Madison stammered. "I'm sorry. I didn't mean to say—"

"Forget it," Aimee said, puckering her lips again to distribute the lip gloss evenly. She slung her bag over one shoulder. "Just forget I said anything, too."

With that, Aimee turned and headed in the opposite direction, toward her next class.

"Wait!" Fiona called out. "Aim, I have the same class as you!" Fiona took a deep breath. "Want me to talk to her?" she asked Madison.

"About what?" Madison said. "The fact that I just said the dumbest thing ever?"

Fiona shrugged. "Don't worry so much. She'll get over it. See you guys at lunch?" she said.

"Bye, Fiona!" Lindsay called out. She moved closer to Madison. "Don't worry about Aim right now," she said. "You have a mystery to solve, remember?"

Madison smiled. "I guess."

"We should go to social studies class," Lindsay said. "If we're late, Mrs. Belden will throw a fit."

The day passed quickly.

Aimee had dance practice and didn't show up in the cafeteria at lunchtime, so Madison had no chance to apologize or talk or make things right in any way between them. Maybe it was just better to let things blow over, Madison decided, so she didn't leave any notes in Aimee's locker. She also didn't make plans to e-mail Aimee or see her later.

At the end of the day, Madison went up to the library again to wait until it was time for her flute lesson with Mr. Olivetti.

She sat in the same carrel where she had been the day she'd heard the squeaky voice. But no mysterious people showed up in the library this time. It was just Madison and a couple of other seventh graders working on book reports.

Madison tried to work on a revolutionary–war time line that had been assigned for weekend homework in social studies class, but she couldn't keep her thoughts straight. Mostly, she was still steaming about the fight with Aimee. But Madison had other things on her mind, too.

Today's date was the same as the one that had been shown on the slip of paper she'd found two days before. Should she investigate it? Maybe she could stop off at Marquette Street on the way home after her flute lesson. She could scope out the location. That's what Major DeMille always talked about. It was one of the things real detectives needed to do.

Madison got up and walked around the library. She hoped another clue to the growing mysteries at FHJH would magically appear.

Instead of a clue, however, Madison got the enemy.

She spotted Poison Ivy in a corner of the library, with her nose buried in an encyclopedia. Considering the fact that Ivy hardly ever studied, the chances of Madison running into Ivy up there were about a hundred to one.

And yet there she was.

The suspicious side of Madison thought it must be a sign of something. It was hard not to shake the notion that Ivy was a part of the torn-paper mystery. Otherwise, why did she keep showing up? Madison wondered if Ivy was also responsible for the theft at school. Ivy was known to do anything to get her way. Maybe the "precious object" that the teachers were talking about was a test. Once, in science class, Ivy had cheated on a quiz by copying Madison's paper. It didn't take much of a leap to imagine Ivy stealing a test to get a better grade.

"What are you staring at?" Ivy yelled across the library.

Madison realized that she had, in fact, been staring—and she'd been caught. She wanted to kick herself. Major DeMille would never have let himself be spotted that way while gathering evidence.

"Sorry," Madison said dumbly. "I was just—"

"Where's Hart?" Ivy snapped. "Oh, look. He's not with you! What a surprise—"

"How should I know where Hart is?" Madison retorted. "He's probably playing hockey. What do you care?"

Ivy gathered her books together and stood up. "I have nothing else to say to you, Madison Finn."

Madison didn't know how to respond. Ivy was good at leaving her speechless.

Madison sat down on a bench by the large library windows and gazed out onto the back lot behind the school. Way out beyond the teachers' parking lot there were wide, open fields and a forest. The land looked like a quilt of color; it curved and dipped.

Those were the far hills of Far Hills.

They looked inviting from way up here, Madison thought.

She wondered how many mysteries were hidden in those hills.

Madison looked up at the clock on the wall; it read 3:02. Realizing she was late for her lesson, she sped out of the library and down the staircase to Mr. Olivetti's room. For the first time maybe ever, he wasn't late. Mr. Olivetti was waiting, tapping his conductor's baton on his desk as he read through a pile of papers.

"Sorry!" Madison cried as she burst through the door, flute case in hand.

Mr. Olivetti looked up, a sad expression on his face. "Oh!" he said, surprised. "Sit-a-over there," he said.

There was something different about the way he was acting, Madison thought instantly. He kept dropping things. And he was chewing on his nails, a nervous habit that Madison had only noticed in him once or twice before.

Later, out of the blue, somewhere in the middle of her practicing scales, Mr. Olivetti sat down on a chair and declared, "I cannot go-a on."

Madison stopped playing. "Are you okay?" she asked.

His eyes darted from one side of the room to the next. "Yes, I'm-a . . . I'm-a-fine, Miss Madison."

Madison didn't believe him. She remembered what Lindsay had said about possibly having over-heard Mr. Olivetti in the teachers' lounge. She couldn't resist the opportunity to ask him about it.

"Are you absolutely, positively sure you're okay?" Madison asked again.

"I have a lot on-a-my mind, that's all," Mr. Olivetti said.

"Did you hear anything about a robbery at school?" Madison asked.

Mr. Olivetti's eyes grew wide. "Robbery?" he echoed. "What about robbery?"

"I heard that there was a robbery somewhere," she responded matter-of-factly.

"I don't-a-know what you are-a-talking about," Mr. Olivetti said.

His stare landed on Madison, and she felt as if he were looking right through her, boring little holes in her with his dark eyes. Madison wasn't sure what was going on, but it made her squirm a little.

Did Mr. Olivetti have something to do with the robbery?

After that, he stared at the clock and rubbed his chin as Madison completed her exercises. Watching him made it nearly impossible for her to focus on the flute.

He acted the way Madison imagined a guilty person would act, all strange and sweaty. What if all of the blame for the school theft were placed on a student when, really, the one responsible for the crimes was a teacher . . . *her* flute teacher!

When the lesson ended, Madison hoped Mr. Olivetti would say more about the robbery—or give himself away in some other manner.

Were there other clues to his guilt right there in the music room?

Eyes and ears OPEN.

That was what the *Crime Time* Web site always advised.

Madison quickly glanced around, but all she saw was the usual chairs and tables, music stands, and someone's tuba parked in the corner. Mr. Olivetti's briefcase was propped up against the desk in front of another large black attaché case with the initials *PKO*. Were those his initials? Madison speculated about what was inside the briefcases. But just as she was about to wander over for a sneaky peek, Mr. Olivetti shooed her out of the classroom.

"Hurry up, my dear. Next lesson coming in!" he cried, mopping his brow.

Wow, Madison thought to herself. He's so nervous he really is sweating. That has to mean something.

As Madison walked out of the room, the next music student wandered in, carrying a guitar. The wall clock said it was a few minutes after four o'clock.

Madison remembered the mysterious scrap of paper.

Friday at 4 @ 411 Marquette Street.

Madison got a whirly feeling inside her belly, as if something weirder than weird was about to happen. She returned to her locker and got the books she needed for doing homework over the weekend. Then she left the school, walking home via Marquette Street—just in case.

When Madison saw the familiar street sign, she could felt her pulse thump. She wasn't sure if she should walk by 411 Marquette just to see if there was anything suspicious. But she did anyway.

It was a warm afternoon, and the sidewalks along the walk home were surprisingly busy. Kids buzzed around on scooters, other kids marched by carrying wrapped gifts, and parents dropped kids off by the curb. There didn't seem to be anything mysterious going on there.

At least, not at first.

Madison approached Number 411 from the opposite side of the street. She recognized some of the faces of people passing by. A kid she knew from Mrs. Wing's school Web site committee was headed straight for the front door of Number 411. She wanted to grab him and ask what was going on. But she stopped herself. There were other kids who looked familiar heading toward the house, too, but they were all older than Madison. They were all ninth graders, Madison guessed.

Maybe Aimee had been right. Maybe it was better not to snoop around like this. She didn't belong there. Madison hoisted her orange bag onto her shoulder and headed for home—for real.

"Maddie? Is that you?"

Madison's heart stopped. She turned to see Mariah Diaz, Egg's older sister, standing there on the sidewalk outside 411 Marquette Street with another girl. Mariah was in the ninth grade at FHJH.

"Oh, wow! What are *you* doing here?" Mariah asked.

Madison had to think of something—fast.

Chapter 8

"Um . . . I was on my way home," Madison said; it was mostly true.

"That's cool," Mariah said, not really seeming to care that Madison was standing there.

"You dyed your hair again," Madison said.

Mariah had a purple streak running down the side of her face. Her hair was pulled back into a fuzzy, leopard-patterned hair clip.

"Yeah, my mom was ready to kill me when she saw it. She almost made me dye it black like the rest of my hair. Oh, by the way, this is Penelope," Mariah said, introducing her friend.

Penelope had bright orange hair that was pulled back in a ribbon. Madison recognized her from the halls at school.

"Hi," Madison said.

"You're in Walter's class, right?" Penelope said, using Egg's real name. "I think I've seen you around."

Madison wanted to answer, but she couldn't. She could barely *think*. When Penelope asked the question again, Madison still couldn't respond. It was as if her brain had just stopped working.

There was a good reason for it.

"Maddie, what is wrong with you?" Mariah asked. She snapped her fingers in front of Madison's face. "Hello?"

"You look like you saw a ghost or something," Penelope said.

Indeed, Madison felt as if she had seen a ghost—or at least *heard* one.

Penelope was the owner of the squeaky voice from the library. Madison was sure of it.

She eyed Mariah's friend up and down, from her faded jeans to the black portfolio case she held in her left hand. Madison looked down at Penelope's feet, too. There they were: the pink-laced sneakers from the library.

Madison didn't know what to say.

"Knock-knock," Mariah teased. "Is anyone home?"

Madison snapped out of her daze with a gasp. "What did you say?" she replied.

Mariah laughed out loud. "Maddie, you've acted

weird sometimes," she said, "but this takes the cake. I asked you if anyone was home. Obviously *not* . . ."

Penelope kept smiling. "Do you like my shoes?"

"Your shoes?" Madison said.

'Yeah, you're staring at my feet," Penelope replied with a chuckle.

"Oh, no . . ." Madison stammered. "Am I? I have the same sneakers," she lied.

"What are you doing here anyway, Maddie? This is a ninth-grade party. Did someone from my class invite you?" Penelope asked.

"No . . . I . . . I . . ." Madison said. Her mind raced. "I was on my way home. I just stopped to see what was going on. It's a party, huh? I didn't know."

Penelope's voice still had that familiar squeak. "Yes! A surprise party! Only, we're late, I think. It started at four. Isn't that dumb that we got here late, so we'll miss the best part? Well, maybe next time, right?"

Madison nodded. "Right," she said.

"You know Maddie, Penelope is in the school music ensemble. Aren't you?" Mariah asked.

"Sort of," Madison admitted. "But I have a lot of flute practicing left to do before I can ever perform."

"You play flute? That is so cool. I play piano!" Penelope kept right on squeaking. "Mr. Olivetti is a super teacher, don't you think?"

"Sure," Madison said.

"You know, I like that hair clip a lot," Penelope said, still acting overly nice.

Why was she acting so nice?

Madison reached up to see which clip she had in her hair. It was a tortoiseshell barrette. "I like your head-band," she told Penelope. "That's a cool bag, too."

"It was my mom's or grandmom's or something. It's a hand-me-down," Penelope explained. "I carry it everywhere with me."

The longer she looked at it, however, the more Madison realized that Penelope's black bag looked familiar. In fact, it looked an awful lot like the black case Madison had seen earlier in Mr. Olivetti's office.

Then she noticed the initials on the side of Penelope's bag: *PKO*.

Her heart sank.

That was *exactly* what Madison had seen on the bag in Mr. Olivetti's classroom.

What was Penelope doing with it?

Gramma Helen had always told Maddie to trust her gut feelings—and something big was gnawing at Madison's gut. From that moment in the library when she found the paper, Madison had known that something strange was going on. Now she'd located the girl with the squeaky voice—and Penelope was carrying suspicious cargo.

This was no case of mistaken-bag identity.

This had to be Mr. Olivetti's bag!

Where was a crime-scene photographer when

Madison needed one? Right there was the evidence she needed in order to prove that something mysterious was going on at FHJH. What if this bag were the connection among the party, the scrap of paper, and the thefts at school?

Madison wished she could have asked the real Major DeMille for advice. *Ask questions. Expect answers.* That was what he always said on *Crime Time.* That's what she would try to do.

"Your bag is so big," Madison said. "Isn't it hard to carry everywhere? Why did you bring it to a party? What's inside?"

"What are you, Maddie, the Inquisition?" Mariah asked. "It's just a dumb bag. Come on, Pen, let's go. We're late."

"Sorry." Madison realized she had gone a little overboard with the questions. "Um . . . It was good to see you," she said to Mariah. "And to meet you," she told Penelope.

"Totally!" Penelope said, still smiling.

Maybe she was being nice in order to hide something?

Mariah leaned in toward Madison before walking away and whispered, "Are you okay? You seem kind of . . . I don't know . . . strange."

"I'm okay." Madison said.

Mariah and Penelope waved as they walked into 411 Marquette Street and the party. Madison waved back. She watched Penelope lift the black bag onto her shoulder and enter the house.

Maybe she was carrying other things that she'd stolen from the school, Madison thought. Or maybe she'd stolen stuff from other places, too. Or maybe . . .

Wait! a voice cried inside Madison's head. Her thoughts were spinning out of control. She'd only met Penelope two minutes ago, and she already had her pegged as the great criminal of Far Hills. Major DeMille would have said that that wasn't so smart. Madison could almost hear his voice.

A good detective would wait to gather stronger evidence before flinging around random accusations.

So Madison needed more evidence. She had to be 100 percent sure Penelope's bag and Mr. Olivetti's bag were one and the same.

Madison walked on toward home as quickly as she could, stopping only once, to tie her shoelaces.

When she arrived at her house on Blueberry Street, Mom and Phin happened to be outside on the front porch, watering the mums in the planters that lined the porch steps.

"Rowwrororrooooo!" Phin barked when he saw Madison.

Madison dropped her bag on the sidewalk and ran to pick him up. His curlicue pug tail was wiggling fast.

"How was school?" Mom asked as Madison grabbed her stuff again and climbed onto the porch.

"Fine," Madison said, sounding as noncommittal as possible. She wasn't sure she was ready to tell Mom about the day's super snooping just yet. Madison needed more evidence to solve the crime and to prove to Mom that her detective work was the real deal.

"How did the math test go?" Mom asked.

"Math test?" Madison said with a blank look.

Mom laughed. "Yes, the one you said you were up all night studying for!" Mom exclaimed. "Was it hard?"

Madison gulped. She'd told Mom the night before that she had been studying. That way she'd been able to chat online and send e-mails for a longer while.

"It was a breeze," Madison lied.

"Good," Mom said. "You had a flute lesson this afternoon, too, right?"

Madison nodded. "It was good," she said.

"See where all this hard work gets you?" Mom said. "I'm so proud of you!"

Madison thought about her sleuthing. Where would *that* hard work get her? She patted Phin on the head but then went indoors without him. He was staying outside in order to go for an evening walk with Mom. Madison went upstairs and set herself up in front of her laptop. Since she had been able to finish two of her assignments during a free period, Madison didn't feel as guilty about jumping online before finishing the rest of her homework.

No sooner had she logged on and started to surf around than an Insta-Message appeared in a corner of the screen.

```
<BalletGrl>: WHere were u after
   school???
```

Madison was happy to hear from Aimee, especially after they'd shared a bad moment in the hall earlier that day. But she also knew she couldn't tell Aimee what she had *really* been doing after school.

```
<MadFinn>: nothing
```

Aimee asked Madison to go to a private chat room called DANCRS. Madison met her there.

```
<BalletGrl>: Sorry about 2day
<MadFinn>: me 2
<BalletGrl>: I know I acted a little
   krazy
<MadFinn>: :-(((
<BalletGrl>: I'm over it already
   don't worry
<MadFinn>: I know that was SUCH a
   wrong thing 4 me 2 say. I'm
   sorry!!!!
```

```
<BalletGrl>: QW I understand y u got
   upset
```

She understood? Madison was relieved to hear that. Maybe Aimee would understand if Madison explained the new mystery she was trying to solve?

Madison typed quickly.

She told Aimee about the scrap of paper, Mr. Olivetti's odd behavior, and Penelope. Of course, Madison was careful (as any good detective would be) to use only initials when referring to her "suspects" online.

Aimee took a moment to write back.

```
<BalletGrl>: r u kidding me? That is
   so weird
<MadFinn>: plus I think P. is
   stealing things from school I
   swear she is b/c she was acting
   WAY too nice
<BalletGrl>: u think she's guilty b/c
   she is nice and wears sneakrs with
   pink laces?
<MadFinn>: and she has Mr. O's bag
   don't 4get!
<BalletGrl>: u can't suspect people
   with only that can u? Maybe she's
   just being nice.
<MadFinn>: I know it's not a lot of
   evidence but
```

<BalletGrl>: sounds 2 me like maybe ur jumping to conclusions a little

<MadFinn>: u really think so? I just have this gut feeling

<BalletGrl>: yeah but gut feelings don't convict criminals on Crime Time do they?

<MadFinn>: no but

<Balletgrl:> maybe ur mystery obsession is making u a little paranoid now 2 like the whole world is guilty or something

<MadFinn>: it is not like that y do u say THAT

<BalletGrl>: u really xpect me 2 believe that there's some school conspiracy and people r stealing bags it sounds so dumb

<MadFinn>: not people stealing bags just 1 person P. and how can u say it's DUMB

<BalletGrl>: it seems dumb that's all sorry

<MadFinn>: WELL YOU ARE DUMB

Madison couldn't believe she'd actually typed the words, but she had—in all caps, too. And she had hit SEND very quickly.

It was way too late to take it back now.

Madison waited, tapping her fingers on the

keyboard. Aimee must have gotten Madison's last post. Why hadn't she responded yet?

```
<MadFinn>: Aim?
```

Madison chewed on her lower lip and waited a little bit longer. She knew her BFF was still online. <BalletGrl> was still in the chat room. But no one was writing back anymore.
This wasn't good.

```
<MadFinn>: Aim? I'm sorry again. I
    didn't mean that. AIM?
```

Madison took a deep breath.
Then she saw Aimee's screen name pop up at last.

```
<BalletGrl>: *poof*
```

Aimee was gone? Just like that? Madison flipped. She raced to Mom's room for the portable phone and dialed Aimee's phone number, but all she got was a busy signal. Of course! The Gillespies didn't have a separate line for the computer as Madison did. Aimee was obviously still online.

Madison thought about heading downstairs and grabbing Phin. They could walk over to Aimee's and meet up with her, Blossom, Yin, and Yang. A long walk with the dogs present could clear everything up. Madison could apologize in person for saying two obnoxious things to her friend in the space of only one day.

But then Madison remembered that Mom was already out with the dog—and it was getting pretty late, anyway. Plus, there was a new episode of *Crime Time* on. Madison couldn't miss the beginning of that, could she? Not with everything that had happened that day. A good detective needs to brush up on her crime-solving skills. Madison needed some serious help with her clues.

So Madison chose TV over BFF.

After all, there was no harm in waiting until the next day to sort things out with Aimee . . . was there?

Chapter 9

Friday night's *Crime Time* episode was one of the best Madison had ever seen. She felt bad about not talking to Aimee, but she was glad she'd stayed home to watch her show.

The new episode was titled "Red-Handed," and it profiled a woman who had traveled cross-country hijacking cars and committing petty crimes for a while, but had then gotten into identity theft, credit card fraud, and a whole bunch of other crimes. The woman's name was Frosty Smith, or at least, that was her name while she was on the lam. It turned out that the name was merely an alias. Frosty's real name had been Myra Limp. Madison couldn't believe any of the names were real.

Her mind danced around the idea of creating aliases.

What if Penelope, Mariah's friend, wasn't using her real name? What if she was just posing as a student at FHJH so she could commit crimes? Madison knew that that wasn't even close to being true, but it was fun to think about. It was exciting to imagine being in the middle of an international intrigue, just like people in the movies and on *Crime Time*.

And what would Madison's own alias be? She thought hard.

Charlotte Helena Isobel Marguerite Phoebe Antoinette?

Those were just a few of Madison's favorite girl names, combined as one.

Madison turned up the volume on the TV when it came time for Major DeMille's wrap-up of the show. This time he took live calls from viewers. Madison loved watching him work the bank of *Crime Time* phones. He would walk up and down the aisles at the soundstage where the show was filmed, stopping to answer callers phoning in to the switchboard. He looked like such a hunk, strolling back and forth in his gray V-neck sweater and his jeans. Major DeMille was hotter than hot.

"Madison?" Mom was at the doorway to the living room, where Madison was watching her show. "Planning to go up to bed anytime soon?" she asked.

Madison moaned. "Mom, the show is almost over. I'll go up in a minute."

"You said that ten minutes ago. Come on, Madison."

Luckily, the closing credits for *Crime Time* flashed on-screen. Madison didn't put up much of a fight. She headed upstairs, brushed her teeth, slipped into her pajamas, and collapsed onto her bed—with laptop in hand. As soon as Mom had shut the door for the night, Madison went online.

She quickly connected to bigfishbowl.com and then onto her e-mailbox again. Madison had no new messages. But she did have one in mind that she needed to write.

```
From: MadFinn
To: Bigwheels
Subject: Being a Detective
Date: Fri 15 Oct 9:27 PM
Did u see what Major was wearing on
the show tonite? I think that was
maybe my fave outfit ever. He got
a haircut 2 and it looks good. I
wonder if he has a GF?

FYI: This snooping around is
harder work than I thought. First
of all, it's hard to act cool
when ur collecting clues. I can
be a little clumsy sometimes and
```

noisy too, even when I'm trying 2
be quiet.

Mostly it's hard 2 deal w/friends
when they don't understand how
important it is 2 me 2 be a
detective. Did u ever do something
fun and ur friends just didn't get
it? Earlier tonight Aimee went
offline when we were chatting w/o
even saying a word. I'll try not to
dwell on it but she really bugs me.
I always support her dance and stuff.
Y can't she support me? :-S

N e way, I'm making progress on my
latest case. I think I have a prime
suspect and I just need more
evidence. More on that 18r. Here's
a :-{} for you!!!

Yours till the moon lights,

MadFinn

Madison hit SEND. Then she checked her buddy
list. Her only friend online at the moment was Fiona.
Madison sent her a message and they escaped into a
chat room called WETWINZ, the same as Fiona's
screen name on bigfishbowl.com.

\<Wetwinz\>: what r u doing tonite did u watch ur show?

\<MadFinn\>: OC! One of my fave episodes

\<Wetwinz\>: Mom wouldn't let me watch she hogged the TV tonite to watch some show about the old west. ZZZZZZ

\<MadFinn\>: I think I'm a CTA!

\<Wetwinz\>: What is that?

\<MadFinn\>: Crime Time Addict LOL

\<Wetwinz\>: did u talk to Aim tonite?

\<MadFinn\>: yes what did she tell u

\<Wetwinz\>: nothing I can't get her on the phone the line is always busy and she's not online it's weird

\<MadFinn\>: oh

\<Wetwinz\>: BTW I have big gossip 4 u from Chet actually about what Lindsay overheard the other day

\<MadFinn\>: what? Tell me!

\<Wetwinz\>: Chet sez he knows what was stolen at school. some ninth grader told him it was sheet music or something else it doesn't sound very important

\<MadFinn\>: Sheet music?

\<Wetwinz\>: not ordinary sheet music though, it was really really old and worth a lot of money

\<MadFinn\>: where was it stolen?

\<Wetwinz\>: Mr. Olivetti's room. I
think he had it in this black case
and it went missing.

\<MadFinn\>: Mr. Olivetti? He had it in
a BLACK case????

\<Wetwinz\>: Didn't u have a flute
lesson w/him 2day?

Madison was in shock.

She quickly finished up her conversation with
Fiona so she could open a file and write some notes.
The mystery from school was starting to make a lot
more sense. Madison's theories about Mr. Olivetti
and Penelope could have been right!

She opened a new file.

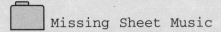 Missing Sheet Music

Aimee is so wrong. I can totally figure
out the mess with the thefts @ FHJH. I am
already making MAJOR progress, or should I
say MAJOR DEMILLE progress?

Facts:

• Mr. Olivetti has a black bag. Penelope
has the identical black bag with initials
PKO that stand for something-something-
Olivetti, obviously! Duh!

• Penelope knows Mr. Olivetti because
she plays piano with him and is in
ensemble. She had a BIG opportunity to
steal the bag.

• Penelope is Miss Squeaky Voice. I know it!!!

• Penelope said the words "sheet music" in the library when I was listening. She must have been talking about the stuff she stole!

• Penelope is way too nice to really be nice. She is hiding something.

<u>Stuff I Need To Know</u>:

• Who was in the library with Penelope when I heard them?

• Is Ivy involved in this? Is Mariah?

• Why does Mr. Olivetti say he knows nothing about a robbery?

• What's in the black bag?

Madison shut down her laptop and closed her eyes. She tried to go to sleep, but it was hard to do. The room was filled with moonlight that cast an eerie glow on the walls and chairs. Even with the shades down, it seemed as though a lamp had been turned on. There wasn't a lot Madison could do, except maybe hide her head under the covers. When Phin trotted across the room to get a drink from his dish near Madison's closet, he cast a shadow on one wall that made him look five times his size.

"Come here, Phinnie," Madison called out to him when he'd finished drinking. He hopped up onto the bed, and she began to stroke his head, and soon, despite the bright light, they both fell fast asleep.

* * *

"Good morning, Maddie!" Fiona chirped into the phone on Saturday morning.

A groggy Madison could barely reply. "Morning," she mumbled. She wasn't sure if it was the moonlight in her room the night before or all the thoughts about the sheet-music mystery that had her feeling extra tired.

"Aimee is coming over in an hour. We're making cookies," Fiona said.

"For who?" Madison asked.

"For us!" Fiona said. "So why don't you come over in an hour, too?"

Madison sighed. "I don't know if that's a good idea," she said.

Fiona was clearly confused—and clearly out of the loop on the whole Madison-Aimee argument.

"Why isn't it a good idea?" Fiona asked. "I thought it was a *great* idea. We haven't hung out together on the weekend in a while. Besides, my brother is out of the house all day. Since he got into trouble, Dad is making him run errands, and he can't bring his Game Boy or anything."

"Well," Madison sighed again. "I guess I'll come over."

She hoped that Aimee wouldn't mind—and that Aimee would actually speak to Madison once they all got to the Waterses' house.

An hour later, after helping Mom rake some leaves in the front yard and taking Phin for a long walk around the neighborhood, Madison arrived at Fiona's doorstep. As she waited for Fiona to answer the bell, Aimee came up behind her.

"Hi," Aimee said.

"Hi," Madison said.

They both looked at each other. Madison hit the doorbell again.

"I'm sorry, okay?" Madison said, half apologetic and half defensive. She couldn't help herself.

"Yeah," Aimee said, kicking at a loose pebble on the Waterses' porch. Aimee leaned over and hit the doorbell again herself.

All at once the door flew open. Fiona stood there in tears.

"Oh, my God!" Aimee exclaimed.

"What's wrong?" Madison asked.

"Come inside," Fiona sobbed. "I feel like I'm going to pass out."

The three pushed their way into the front hall. Fiona seemed to be at home alone.

"Let's go up to my room," Fiona cried. "I brought some juice and snacks up there so we could talk. . . ." She dissolved into tears again.

"Fiona!" Madison said, feeling a little choked up at the sight of her friend's emotional outburst.

"Fiona, what is the matter? Tell us!" Aimee said.

They went up to Fiona's room, where all three collapsed onto the floor. "It's Egg," Fiona sobbed some more. "He hates me! *Hates me!*"

"What?" Madison asked with disbelief. "No, he does not hate you. That's ridiculous."

"Why do you say that he hates you?" Aimee asked.

"We had a fight," Fiona said.

At almost the exact same time, Madison and Aimee said, "Ohhhh."

"It was a *big* fight, too," Fiona continued.

"What did you fight about?" Aimee asked.

"I don't remember," Fiona said.

"What?" Aimee said. "How can you not remember? Didn't you just have the fight?"

"Yes, but I'm so upset," Fiona said. "I just forgot. Something about how I always overreact if he doesn't call me back or E me back right away."

"Well, you know how Egg is, Fiona. He'll get over it." Madison said. "So will you. Haven't you had this fight before?"

"I never want to see him again!" Fiona said dramatically.

"You don't mean that," Aimee said.

"I'm returning his sweater that he loaned me, and I'm returning his stupid book on computers, and I'm definitely not going to that stupid movie this week, either," Fiona ranted.

Madison gasped. "What are you talking about?" she asked. "You can go to the movie with us. You don't need Egg. You can go with me and Aim—"

Fiona shook her head fiercely. "No way."

"Well, I wasn't going, anyhow," Aimee reminded Madison.

"You guys can't *both* bail out of going to the movies! That isn't fair," Madison said.

"Isn't fair for who?" Aimee asked. "Can't you make goo-goo eyes at Hart if you go by yourself?"

Madison's jaw dropped.

Fiona stopped crying instantly.

"That is so mean," Madison said.

"Well, it's true," Aimee said.

As upset as Fiona had been, she now realized that she needed to switch gears. She needed to keep the peace.

But it was too late.

"We don't all have to go to the movies just because you want to go," Aimee said. "We don't all automatically like the things you like."

"Huh?" Madison said feeling flustered.

"Aim . . ." Fiona tried to step in.

"And why *aren't* you going on Wednesday to the movies?" Madison asked.

Aimee shrugged. "I told you why. Because I don't want to see some dumb detective movie."

"Detective movies are not dumb!" Madison cried.

"You mean they're not dumb like *me*?" Aimee snapped back.

"I told you I was sorry about saying that before. . . ." Madison said. "Aimee, this isn't fair."

Aimee rolled her eyes. "What isn't fair?"

"Stop being mad at me!" Madison declared.

"Should we bake some cookies now?" Fiona asked meekly.

Aimee looked over at Fiona. "Cookies?"

Madison giggled. "That's a great idea, Fiona. Bake cookies."

"Well, what am I supposed to say?" Fiona asked aloud. She still sounded sniffly. "I feel like a referee lately!"

"Oh, Fiona, I'm sorry," Aimee said first.

Madison apologized, too. "Maybe baking cookies isn't such a bad idea after all," she added.

They headed down to Fiona's kitchen together, and for the moment, things felt peaceful again.

But Madison knew the truth.

On the surface, things were all cookie batter and smiles, but underneath, something still felt wrong between her and Aimee.

It was like a BFF mystery.

And Madison wasn't sure she was up to solving it.

Chapter 10

On Sunday, Madison and Aimee didn't really talk, either on the phone or online. Madison worried that Aimee was still angry. So when Monday morning rolled around, she searched the school hallways for her BFF. She needed to make things right—100 percent right.

The problem was, Madison couldn't find Aimee outside the girl's restroom or in front of their lockers. And she wasn't at early lunch, either. Someone said Aimee was out sick. But Madison didn't know if she could believe *that*.

Was Aimee just avoiding her?

Outside Mrs. Wing's computer classroom, Madison looked up and down the hall for Aimee as she waited for the bell to ring. Everyone gathered around the door waiting for the students from the previous class period to exit the room.

Egg bounced up to Madison and slapped her on the back. Drew stood nearby.

"Lost?" Egg said as he teasingly slapped Madison again.

"Please don't hit me," Madison groaned.

"That wasn't a hit. It was a friendly tap," Drew said.

Egg gave Drew a high five when he said that.

"Aw, you're both so lame," Madison said with disgust.

"Huh? Why am I lame?" Egg asked.

"Actually, you are the lamest," Madison said.

"Hey! What's wrong with you?" Egg said.

"You and Fiona had a fight, right?" Madison asked.

"Not really," Egg said. "And anyway, we made up already."

"Oh, I didn't know you made up. I guess I'm misinformed," Madison said sarcastically.

"Misinformed? Brain-dead is more like it," Egg joked. Drew was laughing, too. "Actually, wait a minute! I think I have your dead brain right here. . . ."

Egg pointed to some dried gum on the bottom of his sneaker.

Madison let out a huge sigh of exasperation. "You make me crazy!" she cried. "Both of you!"

"Leave me out of this!" Drew said.

Egg was already on to the next subject.

"My sister said she saw you last Friday," Egg said.

"I bumped into her and her friend on the side-walk. They were going to a party," Madison said.

"What were you doing there?" Egg asked.

Madison avoided his question. "Do you know Mariah's friend Penelope?" she asked instead.

"You mean the squeaky freak?" Egg said, cackling a little. Drew laughed again, too.

"That's mean!" Madison said, although she couldn't help laughing, too.

Egg was right. Penelope *was* squeaky and she *was* a little freaky. Madison guessed that it was those qualities that made her a likely suspect. Unfortunately, being "freaky" didn't qualify as hard evidence. Madison would have to keep searching for answers elsewhere.

"Egg, did you ask your mom if you could come to the movies this week?" Drew asked, elbowing Egg in the side.

Egg nodded. "She said yes. I told you!"

"What about you, Maddie?" Drew asked.

Madison nodded. "Absolutely. I really want to see *Curse of the Diamond*."

"Fiona's coming," Egg added with a satisfied look. "She told me her mom okayed the day. Chet's coming, too."

Madison waited for some word on whether Hart, too, had confirmed his attendance at the movie afternoon, but none came.

Mrs. Wing pushed open the classroom door and the departing class of eighth-grade students flooded into the hall. As the crowd filtered out, Egg, Drew, and Madison pushed their way inside, where Mrs. Wing had written out the class work on the board. It was a free day. Everyone worked on an assigned topic that helped him or her to tackle Internet problems or surf the Web for information.

The day's topic had Madison doing a happy double take.

Written across Mrs. Wing's chalkboard were two questions.

Where are the best places to look for online information?

How can the Internet help us all to be better detectives?

What an omen! Madison thought. She couldn't believe that that subject was coming up that day, of all days. Being a detective was *in*.

"I'm going to check out the FBI Web site!" Drew announced.

"That's so cool," Egg said. "I'm going to try a search engine."

As excited as she was by the topic, Madison just stared at her computer. Finally, she typed in the Web address for *Crime Time*. It was the ideal place in which to get tips on being a detective. Madison could do the assigned class work *and* read about old *Crime Time* episodes at the same time (as long as Mrs. Wing wasn't looking, of course).

As she surfed the *Crime Time* site, Madison's brain buzzed with theories on the school theft. Madison knew that Penelope seemed guilty, but she also knew that Mr. Olivetti seemed nervous, as if maybe he were guilty, too. It had turned into a plot right out of a TV mystery movie. The thief could be *anyone*.

After Mrs. Wing's class ended, Madison decided that she needed to start interrogating suspects. First would be Mr. Olivetti. Madison worked up the nerve to confront him that afternoon at her flute lesson. Maybe his music room had more clues hidden in it. She would find out.

Unfortunately, when she showed up outside Mr. Olivetti's classroom, there was no Mr. Olivetti. She spotted a hastily written note taped to the door.

Student! I had an emergency and had to leave the building, so no private lesson. I am sorry. Please reschedule with school secretary.
Thank you.
Mr. Olivetti

Madison tried the door. It was locked.
Drat.
She couldn't believe it. An emergency? Didn't Mr.

Olivetti realize that collecting evidence was the true emergency? She peered into the room through the glass door, hoping some clue would jump out at her.

But the room was dark.

This is awfully convenient, Madison thought as she stood in front of the music room. "I decide to question Mr. Olivetti, and he disappears!"

The longer Madison stood there thinking, the more she began to wonder if maybe—just maybe— Mr. Olivetti himself had something to do with the theft. What if his sudden "emergency" were in fact merely a plan to divert attention while he . . . committed more crimes?

This wasn't just the plot of any ordinary mystery movie of the week. This was way better.

Whatever the case, Madison needed to reschedule her flute lesson. She headed down to the school secretary's office, as Mr. Olivetti had requested in his note. Maybe she could get another lesson tomorrow.

The school secretary at the desk was Dot. She was busy making copies.

"Can I help you?" Dot yelled over the loud hum of the copy machine.

"My name is Madison Finn. I am one of Mr. Olivetti's students," Madison said.

"Oh, yes," Dot said, turning off the copier. "Mr. Olivetti said that he would be sending kids down here to have their music lessons reassigned. Let me see where I put his calendar. Just a sec . . ."

She disappeared into the side room and came out with a datebook.

"Looks like tomorrow is mostly free," Dot said. "Can you do that?"

Madison nodded emphatically. That was perfect. The sooner she could interrogate Mr. Olivetti, the better.

"So, we'll just pencil you in here for three-thirty, okay? Anything else I can help you with?" Dot asked, smiling.

Madison was about to turn and walk away, but she stopped herself.

"Actually, yes, there is something else," Madison said. "I know . . . well, I heard . . . that some very important material was stolen from the school. . . ."

"Oh? You heard?" Dot said.

"Yes," Madison stammered. "And . . . well, I was wondering if you had any more details about the theft. Like, are there any suspects?"

"I'm sorry, Madison, but school policy doesn't allow me to give you any of that information."

"Really?" Madison said. "Well, it's not like I'm asking you to tell me anything important. Can't you tell me a little bit about what happened? I have heard conflicting things and . . ."

"No can do," Dot said, clicking her tongue. "Sorry, sweets. That's not information we make available to students. Once the problem has been resolved, then I am sure Principal Bernard will make everything known to the students."

Madison wanted to scream. How could she be a good detective if she wasn't even able to figure out what it was that she needed to detect? She needed corroboration of the identities of her suspects. She needed the evidence. She needed a way to convince Dot that *she* was more than just any old student. Madison Francesca Finn was the one person who could solve this crime.

"Look, Madison, I'd love to spill the beans," Dot said with a wink. "But the truth is I don't know anything. An investigation with the school panel is strictly hush-hush. So, you'd better be on your way, dear."

Madison hung her head and walked out of the secretary's office. She headed back toward her locker.

As her luck would have it, Ivy was standing nearby. She was going through papers in her bag. Luckily, the drones were nowhere in sight.

"Hello, Ivy," Madison said, trying to be nice as she walked by.

"Why so bummed out?" Ivy asked. "Did Hart just dump you?"

Madison whirled around and stood toe-to-toe with the enemy.

"I'm so sick of you," she growled at Ivy.

"You're sick of me? I'm sicker of you! Just get lost," Ivy snapped.

"*You* get lost," Madison said.

Ivy cracked up. "Oh, you mean lost like *you*?"

"Why are you always following me?" Madison asked.

"Excuse me?" Ivy said with disbelief. "I'm following you?"

"That's right!" Madison said. "Wherever I go, you're there. I think you're following me. I just want you to tell me why!"

Madison chuckled to herself. This was an old detective trick she'd read about on the *Crime Time* site. The trick was to accuse someone of following *oneself*. It was an ideal way to throw people off the trail or smoke criminals out of their hiding places. Madison waited to see what the technique would do to Ivy.

"Follow you? Like I would *ever* follow you!" Ivy said, practically spitting. She tossed her hair and walked down the hall without once looking back.

Madison watched Ivy shake her hips as she took off. For a moment, she wished that Ivy *were* the school thief. It would be a lot of fun to catch the enemy red-handed.

Madison opened her locker and stuffed the homework she needed into her orange bag. She took an extra minute to straighten up the books and other objects inside the locker.

Taped inside the door, Madison saw a teeny photo of Major DeMille that she had downloaded from the Internet. He was smiling.

Madison smiled right back at him. "I'm working

on my suspect list," she whispered to the picture. No one was close enough to her locker to hear.

One by one, Madison convinced herself, she would knock the suspects off the list for good.

She wouldn't stop until she was able to catch the real thief—and prove herself a real detective.

On Tuesday afternoon, Madison was grateful to see that Mr. Olivetti had returned to school for his regular (and rescheduled) lessons.

She put on her detective's thinking cap and approached the music room cautiously. There was work to be done.

"Hello, Miss-a-Madison!" Mr. Olivetti called out. "Have-a-you been practicing your scales?"

Madison nodded. She didn't say much at first. She took her flute out of its case and prepared to warm up. Her plan was to play a few scales, get tired, sit down, take a drink of water, and then start right in on the questioning. She would ask Mr. Olivetti about *everything*.

Ask questions. Expect answers.

She had every last detail planned out to the exact minute.

But Madison wasn't prepared for what actually happened: it was Mr. Olivetti who insisted on sitting down to talk.

"I must-a-tell you what-a-happened to me yesterday," Mr. Olivetti confessed.

Madison was all ears.

"I felt so bad to leave-a-my students like that. But I was too upset to teach anymore. You see, I had some private and valuable materials stolen from me."

"You did?" Madison said, playing it straight.

"Yes, I had this old sheet-a-music," Mr. Olivetti explained. "Ancient papers. A family heirloom. I had the sheets packaged in acid-free paper at the store and picked them up before school one-a-day, but, then, *poof!*"

"*Poof?*" Madison repeated.

"The package-a-disappeared. I think someone-a-took it," Mr. Olivetti said.

"Where did you leave it? On your desk?" Madison asked.

"No, no," Mr. Olivetti said. "I-a-had it in my brief-case."

"Your briefcase? The black one?" Madison asked.

"Yes. You know the black one I-a-carry?" Mr. Olivetti said.

Madison nodded. She was adding up the clues inside her head. But just when she thought she was about to figure everything out, someone barged into the music room.

"Whoops! I thought this was my lesson time," the person said.

Madison blinked when she saw who was standing there.

It was Lana Waldorf.

"Oh, hello, Madison," Lana said meekly. She turned back to Mr. Olivetti. "Um . . . I brought you those papers you needed. . . ."

Mr. Olivetti smiled. "Fine, fine. I think your lesson is in a half hour."

"Oh, I'm sorry," Lana said. As she turned to leave, Lana stared hard at Madison.

Something was going on. Madison could feel it. *What was Lana doing there?*

The wheels inside Madison's head began to churn some more.

Lana had already been caught doing something wrong at the clinic, earlier that week. What if she were up to no good again, right here at school?

Madison's mind raced.

Major DeMille would have said that Lana was a confessed thief who had now been caught at the scene of yet another crime! She *had* to be added to the list of suspects. Right?

"So, where was I?" Mr. Olivetti said.

He continued talking about the missing package as if Lana had never put in an appearance. Madison wasn't really listening to him anymore, though. Her mind was on the suspect list.

Penelope? Maybe.

Ivy? Maybe.

Lana? Maybe.

But Mr. Olivetti?

As he continued talking, it seemed increasingly unlikely to Madison that Mr. Olivetti would have stolen his own sheet music—or even faked its disappearance.

Solving this mystery was a lot trickier than she had thought it would be.

Eventually, Madison returned her thoughts to the flute, and Mr. Olivetti resumed his instruction. He let her stay for a few minutes over her normal time to finish playing a short piece.

On her way out, Madison saw Lana again, sitting on the floor outside the music room. Lana had her books spread around her while she tried to finish homework.

"Hi, Madison," Lana said as Madison walked by.

Madison tried looking into Lana's eyes. Was that a guilty stare coming back at her? There was no way to know. It had been a lot easier to prove Lana guilty when she had had cat hair on her sweater, Madison thought.

Madison said a quick hello and then strolled right past Lana and turned toward the bank of lockers on the first floor. As she walked along, Madison heard whispering from around a corner. She slowed down to listen.

The voice was Ivy Daly's.

"I can't believe I got away with it!" Ivy said.

Madison gasped. Got away with it? Got away with *what*? What was Ivy talking about? Got away with stealing? Was this proof that Ivy had something to do with the theft?

Without thinking, Madison charged around the corner.

"Got away with *what*?" Madison said, confronting Ivy. "What did you do?"

Ivy and the drones were too shocked to speak for a moment. But then, Ivy laughed—and the drones laughed, too.

"Got away with wearing this top, you dummy!" Ivy snarled. "What did you think?"

Madison wanted to melt into the floor. Almost instantly, her palms got sweaty.

Usually, at a time like that, running away was Madison's best option. But now she wasn't able to run. Her feet felt frozen in place.

"Gee, Maddie, are you eavesdropping in the halls?" Ivy asked. "Since when did you become such a snoop?"

Madison still couldn't move—and she couldn't answer the accusation, either. Ivy pronounced *snoop* as if it had been the worst thing in the world.

And it felt as though it were.

"You should mind your own business, Madison," Rose Thorn added.

"Yeah, and keep to yourself, too!" said Phony Joanie.

Poison Ivy shook her head. "Pathetic," she said. "Just pathetic."

As she walked away, hanging her head, Madison felt her chest throb. She hadn't felt so slammed by Poison Ivy and her drones in weeks.

It was humiliating.

And it got Madison thinking.

What if she weren't really cut out to be a detective, after all?

Chapter 11

It was a relief when Wednesday morning came. The last place Madison wanted to be was at school. She'd had her fill of flute, Ivy, and the missing-sheet-music mystery. Most of all, she was beginning to doubt whether she had what it took to be a *Crime Time* sleuth.

Of course, not thinking about the sheet music and her suspect list meant that Madison had to think about other things.

For example, today was the day everyone was going to the movies.

The movies.

Madison wasn't really going alone. She was meeting up with her friends, and they'd all be sitting together as a group. But in her heart, Madison felt alone.

And, as if things didn't look (or feel) bleak enough, Egg called.

"Hey, Maddie!" Egg shouted too loudly into the phone, as he often did. "You're cool with the change in plans, right?"

"What change in plans?" Madison asked.

"Different time, different place," Egg said. "I'm calling because I wanted to know if you were coming in the van with us."

"What are you talking about?"

"Didn't Hart call you?" Egg asked. "I talked to him last night, and he said he would call."

Madison sighed. "No, he didn't call," she said dejectedly.

She couldn't believe that Hart not only hadn't called to ask her to be his "partner" for the group date but he hadn't even called her as a friend, to pass along information.

He must really have a good reason for not wanting to talk, Madison thought.

"I guess I need a ride," Madison said. "Who's going in your car?"

"Me, Fiona, Chet, Dan, and now, Hart," Egg said. "And you, I guess."

Madison's blood began to boil a little. It was bad enough that Hart had not called. But why hadn't Fiona called, either? And how could Fiona have

125

known about arrangements to have Hart in her car pool for the movies—and not told Madison about it?

"Is your mom driving?" Madison asked. Señora Diaz was Egg's mom, but she was also Madison's Spanish teacher.

"Yeah, we're taking the monster," Egg said. "The monster" was Egg's term for the family van. "My sister Mariah will probably come, too."

"Your sister?" Madison asked.

"Yeah, she's coming along as a sort of chaperone," Egg said. "It was my mom's idea."

"Chaperone?" Madison giggled. "Okay. And how is Drew getting there?"

"He's coming with Elaine," Egg said with a snicker. "His dad's driving the two of them."

"Oh," Madison said knowingly. Lately, Drew and Elaine had been inseparable.

"So?" Egg asked. "What's it gonna be?"

"I'm in," Madison said, buoyed by the fact that she would be driving to the movies with Hart and the rest of the group. She didn't have to start off the movie date alone, after all. That was good.

It was a relief to stop thinking about solving crimes for one afternoon. Madison and Phin stood outside her closet contemplating a few bold fashion statements for a trip to the movies.

Faded gray Godzilla T-shirt and painter's pants? Too tomboyish.

Blue sweater set with peasant skirt? Too girly.

Plain, cropped T-shirt with faded jeans and Far Hills sweatshirt?

Madison decided on the last combo. The sky was clouding up, and she didn't want to wear anything too complicated. Getting caught in the rain in this outfit wouldn't spell disaster.

Madison pulled her hair back into a bun and applied some mascara that she had borrowed from Mom's vanity drawer. She wasn't used to wearing makeup, except for lip gloss.

"How do I look, Phin? I have to look good. Do I look good? I have to make an impression," Madison posed in front of the bedroom mirror while Phin lay on the carpet, panting.

An exasperated Madison tore off the sweatshirt and replaced it with a striped, V-neck sweater. She put on a pair of dangling earrings with mixed colored stones and a bangle bracelet that Stephanie had given her.

"That's better," Madison told herself. "I just wish I liked the way I looked. Maybe I need a new wardrobe."

Madison headed downstairs to wait for the arrival of the Diaz minivan. It was actually a large SUV, the kind of car that Aimee's environmentally conscious parents were always complaining about.

She wrote a note to Mom and left it on the hall table.

Mom,

 We left noonish. Egg's mom is driving. Going to Far Hills Multiplex over on Acorn Road. Seeing Curse of the Diamond. It's rated PG-13, but we have a chaperone. Be home later. ILY.
xox
Maddie

A loud honk came about five minutes later. Madison said good-bye to Phin and locked the door.

"Maddie!" Fiona gushed, as soon as Madison stepped into the car. "I meant to call you last night. I am so sorry I didn't!"

Madison shrugged. She said a general hello to everyone else inside.

"Hey, Finnster," Hart said.

Madison saw that the only empty seat in the van was, in fact, next to Hart. He was sitting up front, directly behind the driver.

She broke into a wide smile and hopped in.

"Like I said, Maddie," Fiona continued to gush. "I am so, so, *so* sorry."

Madison turned to her friend, sitting in the middle row, next to Egg. "Don't worry about it, Fiona," she said, acting nonchalant.

While speaking to Fiona, she looked to see who else was in the van.

Up front, next to Señora Diaz, was Chet. He looked nervous stuck up front with a teacher. Even if he was good friends with Egg, being around his Spanish teacher made him uncomfortable.

Señora Diaz was cheery. She had been in meetings all morning at school for the faculty conference. After she dropped the group off, she was heading back to school for another summit, over lunch.

Madison glanced into the back row and saw a streak of purple hair. Mariah waved at her. "Hey, Maddie!" she said. "Remember Penelope?"

Madison almost choked. Next to Mariah sat Penelope, from the party, the street, and the suspect list!

"Hi," Madison said meekly.

Penelope was as sticky-sweet as she'd been the first time Madison had met her. "Hiya!" she squeaked.

"We have two chaperones," Fiona said. "Mariah and Penelope. They're helping us get past the PG-13 watchdog at the movie theater."

"Some of us *are* thirteen," Hart said with a smile.

Dan, who was squished in next to Egg and Fiona and behind Madison, piped up, "We're getting the super-size popcorn when we get there, right?"

"Do you need a chaperone for *that*?" Mariah said.

Everyone in the van laughed. Madison shook her head. Dan was always thinking about what to eat next.

The ride over to Acorn Road and the multiplex took about ten minutes. Everyone kept joking and staring out the van windows as they barreled along on the highway access road toward the multiplex.

"Where's Aimee today?" Chet asked.

"Dance class," Madison said. "You know."

"Bummer," Chet said.

Madison didn't know what to make of that comment. For a fleeting moment she thought maybe Chet sounded *interested* in Aimee.

Madison would have to file that one away for future reference.

"I heard this movie has a cool scene with bugs," Dan said. "I read it on Movie Link."

"I read about that, too," Egg said. "It has something like a billion cockroaches in it. Did you know that cockroaches actually have their own agents?"

"Ewww!" Fiona squealed. "Cockroaches are gross."

"I hate bugs!" Madison said.

"Me, too!" squeaked Penelope from the backseat.

"Kids, we're almost there," Señora Diaz called out as she made a few turns onto some back roads. "I'm taking a little shortcut."

"Oh, Mom," Egg groaned. "You always get lost when you take shortcuts."

"I know where we are," Hart said. "Take a left there."

Madison looked up at her crush with wide eyes. She hoped that she would be sitting with Hart inside the movie theater, too.

When they pulled up in front of the entrance to the multiplex, the group shuffled out of the van. Other kids and their parents were lined up for tickets. Egg and his mom made arrangements to meet after the movie ended, and then she left for her meeting.

A few rumbles sounded off in the distance. A big storm was coming. There was something about dark clouds and lightning and damp air that made Madison feel as though she were a real detective. It was like being inside a movie from the 1940s, the ones Mom called film noirs. Madison remembered watching an old movie on TV once called *The Maltese Falcon*.

As they stood on line waiting for tickets, everyone gossiped about other people in the seventh grade. But Madison didn't feel like gossiping. She was busy dreaming up aliases again. What would her detective name be once she solved the sheet-music mystery? She'd imagined her alias as Charlotte Helena Isobel Marguerite Phoebe Antoinette. But that was a mouthful. She'd have to think up something shorter and easier—fast. Something more like Sam Spade.

What about an acronym of her favorite names? That could do it.

Charlotte Helena Isobel Marguerite Phoebe Antoinette—otherwise known as CHIMPA!

Madison cringed. That sounded like some new addition to the zoo.

She needed something more like a groovy spy's name.

"Hey, Finnster," Hart shook Madison's shoulder gently. "We're going inside."

Madison realized that she'd daydreamed herself all the way out of the line and away from her friends.

"Gee, Finnster," Hart said as they walked inside. "What planet are you on today?"

Madison giggled. "Earth. I swear," she said with a grin.

Then it dawned on her. The perfect detective name had been given to her by her longtime crush.

Finnster.

Glad to meet you, Madison imagined herself saying. *I'm Finnster, Private Eye.*

It was perfect.

"Hello!" someone cried from behind the group. It was Lindsay. She jumped up and down. "I'm so glad you guys waited. Thanks!"

Lindsay had taken the bus from her condominium across town. In many ways, Lindsay was like Madison's honorary BFF, after Fiona and Aimee.

"Hey, Maddie!" Lindsay said, grabbing Madison's arm.

Madison was glad to have a partner of some kind

to enter the theater with, although it wasn't the one she'd hoped for.

"So, we're all here now?" Mariah asked. She and Penelope passed out the movie tickets for the group, courtesy of Drew's mom. Then everyone scuttled into the theater in a pack. They moved together like parts of an octopus. Some tentacles stretched out toward the concession stand, while others just headed straight for the ticket-taker by the escalator.

Madison rode up the escalator next to Lindsay and Chet, who couldn't stop making fun of some funny-looking guy wearing a jester's hat whom he'd seen in the lobby. Madison tried pushing forward, to get a few steps closer to Hart, but Chet wouldn't move. And she didn't want to desert Lindsay, either.

The upstairs lobby overflowed with students who had the day off. Madison couldn't believe how many moviegoers there were! She glanced around at the video screens, showing trailers for upcoming films. There was one called *Making Pointe*. It was about ballet.

Madison stared as a blond girl on-screen did pirouettes and high kicks.

Watching the trailer made her miss Aimee.

What was her BFF doing right now?

Fiona and Egg led everyone into the dark theater, securing their own seats somewhere near the middle. Next to them sat Drew and Elaine. On the outer edges the noncoupled friends sat, boys on one side, girls on the other.

Dan, Chet, and Hart sat together, chomping popcorn and cracking jokes.

Madison sat quietly on the other side, with Lindsay, Mariah, and Penelope.

I wish Aim were here, Madison thought again.

Out of the corner of her eye, Madison tried to get a glance at Hart. He was as far out of reach as a person could possibly be and still be in the same row. Madison could just about see the soles of his sneakers. She had never noticed before that his soles glowed in the dark. Then again, Madison had never sat in the dark with Hart.

Plink!

Madison flinched. Someone had zapped a kernel of popcorn at her head.

Plink!

"Hey!" Madison said softly. "Who did that?"

Fiona couldn't stop laughing.

Egg tattled.

"It was Hart," Egg said. He leaned over toward Madison and whispered so softly that only Fiona could hear. "He did it because he likes you."

Madison gasped. She wanted to run away. If Lindsay hadn't been sitting next to her, she just might have dashed out of the theater and kept on running until she was far, far away from all potential embarrassment.

Plink!

Madison stood up after the third plink. "Hart!" she cried.

Hart looked over. "What?" he asked innocently.

Madison folded her arms in front of her. "Quit shooting popcorn over here," she said.

"It wasn't me!" Hart said.

"It was *me*, Maddie!" Egg said with a huge laugh. Everyone else laughed then, including Hart.

Madison sat right back down again and buried her head in her hands. When it came to her crush, it didn't take much to embarrass Madison Finn.

"Can you guys keep it down?" Mariah said. She glared at her brother. "Egg, cut it out, will you? Leave Madison alone. The movie's about to start."

Madison smiled through the darkness at Mariah. Maybe having a chaperone, especially one who was Egg's older sister, wasn't such a bad thing.

The lights dimmed, and everyone settled back for the movie.

Madison decided that she would spend the entire movie forgetting about the popcorn incident—and pretty much everything else. She wouldn't think about Hart, Aimee, or *anything* except *Curse of the Diamond*.

But then Madison saw something on the floor that caught her attention.

Something sparkled.

A zipper!

135

Over in the darkness, down by Penelope's feet, was the black bag.

The black bag from the other day.

The black bag from Mr. Olivetti's room.

And despite her wishes to forget about her detective work along with everything else that was bugging her, Madison couldn't help wondering if the stolen sheet music was inside that bag.

What would Major DeMille have done?

Before the movie ended, Madison Finn was determined to figure out what was in that bag once and for all.

Chapter 12

In the Bag

I'm so upset. I was this close to seeing
inside Penelope's black bag. THIS close. We
were in the bathroom after the movie and
she left it--OPEN--on the countertop. I
peeked over and saw some papers in there
(and they DID look like sheet music to me),
but then she closed it, threw it over her
shoulder, and walked out. Am I the lamest
detective who ever lived or what?

Rude Awakening: Today I thought catching
Penelope would be easy, but solving this
mystery is definitely NOT in the bag. LOL.

Sometimes it feels like the harder I
try, the harder it gets. Gramma Helen said

something like that to me once. She said, "The more you know, the less you know." I always wondered what she meant by that. But today I understand a little better. I know more details about the crime, but it only means more suspects, more options, more confusion! Who can I turn to for help? If only Major had a hotline for junior detectives like me.

Right now I'm at Dad and Stephanie's apartment. Even with the cast on her arm she's cooking tonight. She's making Indian food from a recipe she said she got off TV on the Wacky Chef Show.

On top of everything else, I'm not only a failed detective, I can't even flirt right. How could I spend most of the movie thinking about the school mystery? Hart and I were FINALLY at the movies together! Even though we weren't sitting close, I still could have figured out a way to talk to him more, right? Why do I get so nervous? Why was Egg teasing me so much? And why is Fiona always so clingy around Egg? And then we came out of the theater and it was pouring RAIN. I should have asked Hart if I could share his umbrella. Instead, I just got all wet.

Maybe Aimee was right after all about not going. The movie wasn't even very good. Of course I had my eyes covered for like ten minutes when the army of cockroaches attacked one of the--

"Maddie?" Stephanie poked her head into Dad's study, which was where Madison was typing on her laptop. She was taking her laptop everywhere these days so she could keep track of all of the evidence and her detective work. Writing made her feel better.

"Hi, there," Madison replied, looking up from the monitor. "What's up?"

"Dinner will be ready in a few. Your dad just ran out to get a bottle of wine. Can you help me in the kitchen?" Stephanie asked. "I made some appetizers for us."

Madison hit SAVE and closed her laptop. She followed Stephanie back into the kitchen.

A plate of mini–vegetable samosas sat in the center of the kitchen counter. Madison grabbed one and took a bite. It was mostly potato and peas. And it wasn't too spicy at all.

"Mmmm," Madison said. She sat up on a stool. "How can I help?"

"I can do most things with my wrist, but not cutting; too awkward," Stephanie explained. "I thought your dad had done it all, but I need these carrots grated for the salad."

"Sure," Madison offered. She jumped off the stool, grabbed the grater, and started in on the bag of prewashed carrots.

"Isn't tonight *Crime Time* night?" Stephanie asked as they prepared the vegetables.

Madison shook her head. "No, the new episodes are on Fridays."

"How is your detective work coming along?" Stephanie asked.

Madison didn't answer. She just shrugged her shoulders.

"Well, that's not too enthusiastic. What's wrong?" Stephanie asked.

"I'm a little stuck with this crime at school," Madison said. "I think I have all these great clues, and either they turn into dead ends or I miss getting what I really need to prove my case."

"Sounds tricky," Stephanie said. "What's the case about?"

"I really shouldn't talk about it, should I?" Madison asked. "Aren't detectives supposed to keep their cases confidential?"

"That depends," Stephanie whispered. "I promise I won't tell a soul."

"Okay, then, I guess I can tell you," Madison said. "There's a thief at school—and I found him . . . er . . . her."

"A real thief?" Stephanie exclaimed. "Wow. How did you find proof?"

"That's just it," Madison said. "I haven't exactly found the proof yet."

"I see," Stephanie said. "Tell me more."

"Someone stole this very old, very rare sheet music from one of the music teachers at school. From my music teacher, Mr. Olivetti, actually. And I know who the thief is. Well, I've narrowed it down to a list of suspects, anyhow. That's what *Crime Time* tells you to do. I want to do it the way they do it on the show."

"I see," Stephanie said again, thoughtfully biting her lip.

Madison handed Stephanie the plate of grated carrots. "What do you think?"

"Thanks for the carrots, Maddie," Stephanie said. "Could you hand me that crushed–pepper olive oil?"

Madison grabbed the huge bottle of oil from the counter and passed it over to Stephanie, who was putting the finishing touches on some salad dressing.

"I think you're off to a good start. Tell me how you made your list," Stephanie said.

"Evidence, obviously," Madison said. "That's what Major DeMille on *Crime Time* looks for: hard evidence. Well, I guess in some ways my evidence is a little soft. But I'm working on it."

"Have you been spending all your time solving this crime?" Stephanie asked. "When do you have time to do homework, or anything else?"

Madison didn't know how to answer. The truth was that she had been getting a little bit behind in all of her subjects since the sleuthing had begun. But she couldn't admit that to Stephanie.

Stephanie was Madison's *stepmother*—and that meant that she had parental privileges now. She had the right to question and comment on things in a different way than she had before she married Dad. For example, if she found out that Maddie's detective work was getting in the way of her grades, she might just tell Madison to stop.

"I get all my homework done first," Madison lied. "*Then* I work on the clues to the mystery. But work always gets done first."

Stephanie smiled. "Just make sure you don't get too consumed by it all, Maddie. Remember what I said before this all started. Sometimes snooping can take you to places where you don't belong—and where you might not want to be."

"Oh, no," Madison insisted. "That's not me at all."

"Tell me more about your prime suspect," Stephanie said. "Maybe I can help you sort out the evidence."

Madison described Penelope and the black bag Penelope had been carrying before the surprise party and at the movie theater earlier that day.

"And you're sure the bag you saw is the one that belongs to Mr. Olivetti?" Stephanie asked.

Madison nodded. "Of course. I saw it sitting in his room with his things."

"Did he say it was his bag? It could have belonged to someone else," Stephanie suggested.

"Oh," Madison said. She had never considered that the bag could have belonged to anyone except Mr. Olivetti.

"You said that Penelope is in ensemble, too, right?" Stephanie asked. "Maybe she was the one who left her bag there after a rehearsal. . . ."

"Gee," Madison said. "I didn't even think of that."

"Is there anyone else in ensemble who could be the thief?" Stephanie asked.

Madison thought for a minute. Stephanie's questions had her stumped. There were probably dozens of other students who had the motives and the opportunity (two of Major DeMille's favorite words) to commit the crime.

The problem was that Madison hadn't looked for them.

She hadn't investigated other possible suspects beyond the ones who had crossed her path: Penelope, Lana, and Ivy. And of course, Ivy wasn't really a likely suspect, but Madison had to put her on the list anyway, because Ivy was always up to no good.

All at once the title of Finnster, Private Eye, didn't seem right anymore. Madison felt that woozy sensation that she always felt before getting really, really emotional.

Stephanie sensed that Madison was upset.

"Oh, Maddie, what's wrong? You're turning purple."

"I'm a big faker," Madison blurted. "What was I thinking? I'm no Major DeMille. It was a joke to think I could do this. How embarrassing. I'm a *faker*!"

"No," Stephanie said. She reached over and put

her arm around Madison's shoulder. "Don't give up. You are not a faker. It ain't over till it's over."

"Easy for you to say," Madison said.

"I have an idea. Why don't you confront Penelope with the bag as evidence? She'll be forced to tell the truth. Who knows? Maybe she is the guilty one."

"How do I do that?" Madison asked.

"Ask her what's in the bag," Stephanie said. "I'm sure you'll be able to see if she's telling the truth or not. Then you'll know whether or not she had anything to do with taking the sheet music. People often give themselves away. If she seems nervous or agitated when you question her—"

"You really *are* a good detective, aren't you?" Madison interrupted.

"I told you. Nancy Drew," Stephanie said with a shrug.

Just then, the front door flew open and Dad rushed inside clutching a bottle of wine and a pint of cherry ice cream, Madison's favorite.

"Where's dinner?" he joked.

"Ready when you are," Stephanie said. "Madison has been a huge help."

Madison smiled.

"Should we tell Dad?" Stephanie whispered in Madison's ear.

Dad looked curious. "What are you two whispering about?"

"Dad, Stephanie and I were talking about my

detective work," Madison said seriously. "I'm on a case at school."

"You're on a case?" Dad asked. His eyes widened. "That sounds serious."

"That's what I said," Stephanie said.

They spent the rest of the evening sharing conjectures about who could have committed the school theft. Stephanie had the best ideas. Dad came up with some theories of his own. Both Stephanie and Dad reminded Madison, however, that she needed to be careful doing her "detective work."

Stephanie's exact words were: "Just don't accuse someone without the evidence—and give people the benefit of the doubt. Don't assume someone's guilty—ever."

By the time Madison left Dad's and Stephanie's for home, she had creeping doubts about her ability to see the thing through to the end.

Could she really solve this crime?

When she got home later that night, Madison started work on another new file.

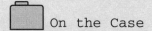 On the Case

Rude Awakening: I feel like a calculator. Everyone's counting on me to solve this mystery . . . and I just don't have a clue.

Well, maybe it's not everyone. Some people are counting on me. And I have a <u>few</u>

145

clues, but they involve actually
confronting people and asking them if
they're guilty and I don't know if I'm up
for that job. I thought being a detective
happened in the shadows. I'm a little more
comfortable there. It's like the play we
did at school. I am way happier being
BEHIND the scenes, not onstage.

The pressure is really on.

I hope that tomorrow I don't blow it.

Chapter 13

Madison woke up earlier than early on Thursday morning. She wasn't hungry, but she headed down into the kitchen anyway. Inside her head she heard a voice say, *So what makes you think you're such a detective, Smarty-Pants?* Madison thought the voice had the distinct ring of Ivy Daly's. Ivy would have said something just that nasty.

There was no time for doubt, Madison thought, trying to reassure herself. She had a case to solve!

Unfortunately, Madison was dying to tell Aimee all about the case so far—and how she felt about it. If only, she thought, Aimee didn't hate mysteries so much. Madison needed her support more than ever. What use was success in anything if you couldn't share it with your best friend in the whole wide world?

Madison had dragged her laptop into the kitchen. Since it was a little while before school, she logged on and sent a quick note to her keypal.

From: MadFinn
To: Bigwheels
Subject: It's D-Day
Date: Thurs 21 Oct 7:17 AM

It's here.

The moment of truth.

D-Day for me (Detective Day).

Thanks for e-mailing me your thoughts about the case. I know you think Mr. Olivetti had something to do with it, but I've decided Penelope HAS to be the guilty one. She has the most evidence (even if it is soft) against her. It had to be her bag, right? No matter what my stepmom says.

So I found out from my friend Egg that his sister Mariah has art class on the second floor at school today around the same time that I have a class up there. So I'm going to wait in the hallway and hope that Penelope

will be by her side like she always
is. Then when the moment is right I
can ask Penelope about the bag. Good
plan, huh? The Crime Time Web site
has a Sneaky Sneak section with
sample questions, so I wrote them
down. I'm channeling Major DeMille
to give me the courage. Will you
please cross your fingers and toes
for me 2?

What do you think? Send me an
e-mail ASAP.

Yours till the case closes,

Maddie

Much later that morning, up on the second floor
at school, Madison followed through with the plan
she'd described to Bigwheels. She pretended to look
at a display cabinet outside the art studio, stalling
for time and hoping to catch sight of Mariah and
Penelope. There were a few moments left before the
second bell rang. Mariah had still not appeared.

Then, out of the corner of her eye, Madison saw
Penelope strutting down the hall. She was alone.
And she was carrying the black bag with her!

Madison couldn't believe her good luck. Not only
was this the perfect opportunity to confront the

suspect, but the suspect had the evidence right there.

"Penelope?" Madison called out, her voice sounding a little hoarse.

Penelope turned.

"Maddie?"

She smiled when she saw Madison. "What are you doing here? I thought this art class was just for ninth graders. Wait—you are in seventh grade, right?"

"I'm not in art class," Madison said quickly.

"Oh," Penelope said, looking a little confused.

Madison had to talk fast. She didn't have much time.

"Um . . . Penelope, can I ask you something?" she asked. "Why do you carry that bag everywhere?"

"This bag?" Penelope frowned. Madison wondered if she were gazing at the face of a guilty girl.

"What is it with you and my bag?" Penelope sighed. "This is, like, the tenth time you've asked me about it," she said.

Madison gulped. "Oh, well . . . I just . . . I just think . . ."

"I mean, why do you carry *that* bag?" Penelope asked. Her sweet voice had turned a bit sour.

"I'm sorry," Madison stammered. She needed to come to the point. Penelope was getting edgy. "I didn't mean to offend you or anything. I just . . . well . . ."

"Well, what? Look. I have to get to class. The bell is about to ring," Penelope said.

"You know about the theft in school?" Madison asked. She couldn't believe she'd said it so plainly.

"Yeah. So? What does that have to do with my bag?" Penelope asked. She didn't bat an eyelash.

Madison's palms felt a little clammy. She needed to see what was inside the bag before she could know for sure that Penelope had had nothing to do with the school crime. The plan wasn't working out as well as Stephanie had said it would. Madison tried to regroup.

"The bag and the theft may be connected," Madison said, trying her best to sound like a real detective. "The sheet music that was stolen was hidden inside something, obviously. A bag fitting your description was spotted near the scene of the crime."

"Oh, my God, who are you? Nancy Drew?" Penelope said.

"No . . . I'm just looking for answers. Can you explain to me why your bag was in Mr. Olivetti's classroom?"

Penelope blinked. "Huh?"

"Tell me the truth. Is this your bag or Mr. Olivetti's bag?" Madison asked seriously.

"Are you kidding me?" Penelope said. "It's my bag. And it was in the music room because I left it there after ensemble rehearsal."

"Um . . . can I see inside the bag, please? Just for a sec?" Madison asked.

"Maddie!" Penelope said. Her face scrunched up so that her eyes turned to slits. "Oh, I get it. You think I stole the sheet music and hid it in my bag? Is that what you think?"

Madison took a breath. Kids passed by in the hallway, knocking into her with their book bags and elbows. It was hot. What was she doing there? What was she thinking? What was she asking?

Madison wanted to run. Run! *Run!*

"I think . . . um . . ." Madison started to explain.

"Look, Madison, there's nothing in my bag but a lot of junk. You can look if you really want to," Penelope said. "But all I have in here is a wadded up T-shirt, some books, and a few pens with no caps on them. . . ."

Penelope opened up her bag and showed Madison its contents, item by messy item.

Madison froze as she reviewed Penelope's things. "That's it? Really?"

"That's all I have in my bag right now. I can't believe you thought I was the one who stole the music," Penelope scoffed. "I mean, I guess I could have stolen it and sold it on the black market," she added with a laugh.

Madison nodded. "I guess—"

"Yeah, right," Penelope said. "Come on!"

The second bell finally rang.

"You know, Maddie, I thought you were so nice before," Penelope said. "But now I'm thinking that

152

maybe I was wrong. Wait until I tell Mariah. . . ."

"No, please, I'm sorry—" Madison started to say, but she stopped. She felt as if she had fuzz on her tongue. She felt unable to say another word.

Penelope turned and headed into the art studio, leaving Madison standing alone in the hallway long after the bell had stopped ringing.

Madison stood there staring at the door to the art room. She stood and stood, staring and rocking on her heels.

"Miss, do you have your hall pass?"

A hall monitor shouted in Madison's face, breaking her trance.

Madison stared at the monitor.

Of course she had no hall pass. But what was worse was the fact that Madison had no criminal.

Penelope wasn't guilty. She hadn't stolen the sheet music. Her bag wasn't Mr. Olivetti's bag. Madison knew the truth now. And so, after all the guessing games, the theories, and the *Crime Time* questions, Madison was right back where she'd started.

Nowhere.

The hall monitor let her off easy. Madison didn't get written up, and she didn't get Detention. Instead, she headed to Mrs. Wing's classroom to help work on the school Web site for the remainder of her free period. There, Madison was able to download photos and material onto the site and try to get her mind off the case, the suspects, and the nonsuspects—at least for a little while.

While she was in the computer lab, Madison tried to access her e-mailbox, but Mrs. Wing came into the room, and the computer froze.

Madison sighed. Finnster, Private Eye, had made the mistake of accusing the wrong suspect. Now, bad luck was following her.

After the free period ended, Madison wandered through the rest of the school day in a fog. She couldn't focus on anything for more than thirty seconds. What was wrong? Her whip-smart detective sensibilities had turned to Jell-O. In the middle of science class, during one of Mr. Danehy's yawn-inducing lectures, she looked down at her notebook to see a list of names she'd scribbled only half consciously.

Madison DeMille
Maddie DeMille
Mrs. DeMille
Finnster DeMille
Madison Jones
Mrs. Jones

Hey! Whoa! NO!
Madison immediately scratched out all the names as well as she could, with a black pen.
Mrs. Jones? She really was in a fog!
Had anyone seen the list? Madison glanced

around the room to make sure that no one was looking over her shoulder.

Ivy Daly was too busy talking to her drones to notice.

Chet was halfway across the room.

And Hart, aka Mr. Jones, had his nose in his science textbook.

Madison breathed a sigh of relief. She tore out the notebook page and ripped it into teeny, tiny pieces. If a Bunsen burner in the classroom had been lit, she probably would have burned the pieces and then washed the ashes down the drain.

How could she have written Hart's name? Madison was letting her guard down. A good detective never did that. She had to find a way to recover.

After class, the last of the day, Madison went back to her locker to retrieve her flute. She'd scheduled another flute lesson for the afternoon. Mr. Olivetti would be waiting.

Originally, Madison had hoped to be able to go to her lesson with good news for Mr. Olivetti about the theft of his old sheet music. She had wanted to pin the crime on Lana or Penelope or even Ivy. But instead, Madison went to her lesson with no suspects at all—except maybe Mr. Olivetti himself. And that was a stretch.

Still.

Madison told herself, stretch or not, that a good detective needed to explore *all* options, including that of considering Mr. Olivetti the guilty guy. It was possible that he'd staged the entire theft in order to collect insurance money or get his name in the papers or win sympathy, wasn't it?

Anything was possible.

Major DeMille would have investigated the music teacher, wouldn't he?

On the way to her lesson, with flute case and bag in hand, Madison decided that she would investigate. She would not give up—not yet. She would do things the Major DeMille way.

The music room was empty when Madison arrived.

It was quiet. A little too quiet.

Then Mr. Olivetti popped out from behind the music-closet door.

"Ah!" he said. "You scared me!"

Madison nearly jumped out of her sneakers, too.

"Miss-a-Finn! I've been expecting you," Mr. Olivetti said.

Something about the way he said that sounded ominous to Madison. Her heart raced. She placed her bag on a chair and opened her flute case.

"Quiet today, aren't we?" Mr. Olivetti said. He fished inside the top drawer of his desk as he spoke. Then he moved over to a file cabinet and started pulling out different files and papers.

"Are you looking for something?" Madison asked.

Mr. Olivetti nodded. "Uh, yes. I am-a-looking for

notes I took at a concert last week. I seem to have mis-a-placed them. . . ."

Madison swallowed.

"Oh?" she said. She steadied herself for further questioning. "Mr. Olivetti?" Madison asked tentatively. "What ever happened to that sheet music that disappeared from your classroom?"

Mr. Olivetti got a blank look on his face. "I told you about that?"

Madison nodded. "Yes, you told me. What happened? Did they ever catch who stole it?"

Mr. Olivetti scratched his nose. He shook his head and stared at the floor.

Madison squirmed as she waited for his response. He was taking a long time to answer, or at least it felt that way. It was like one of those drawn-out moments on *Crime Time*, right before the guilty party confessed to stealing the rubies or robbing the bank. Madison could almost hear the slow, low theme music playing in the background.

Was Mr. Olivetti avoiding Madison's question?

Was this a sign of his guilt?

"Oh, Miss-a-Finn," Mr. Olivetti said, shaking his head. "You got me."

Madison gulped. "I got you?" she stammered. "What do you mean?"

Mr. Olivetti just laughed.

But it sent a shiver down Madison's spine.

Chapter 14

 Case Closed

I don't belong on Crime Time. I belong on that candid video show Gotcha! instead. Even Phinnie is laughing at me.

Mr. Olivetti said "You got me," but he didn't mean "You caught me red-handed!" Sure, he was responsible for the whole sheet-music incident. But not exactly in the way I expected.

Mr. Olivetti didn't steal the sheet music.

He lost it. LOST IT!!!!

Now I'm losing it.

Here's what he told me: he was sure that

the package of sheet music had been swiped
from his classroom. He told the school
administration so they could look into it.
Then everyone started talking. That's when
Lindsay heard about the theft and then Lana
got caught with the cat hair and Penelope
was carrying the bag and my Crime Time
fantasy took over.

Mr. Olivetti said that he had spent the
last week panicked about the missing
package, but that then just that morning
before school he had discovered the sheet
music in its package under the seat of his
car! It was with him the whole time. When
he told me, I just stood there with my jaw
on the floor, gasping for breath. I wanted
to scream, How could you do this to me?!
Of course, he didn't do anything to me,
not really. I did the damage myself. I'm
the one with the overactive imagination,
after all.

Rude Awakening: Be careful or you'll
poke your Private Eye out.

Stephanie tried to warn me about this.
She said that too much snooping could get
me into trouble. And she said I should
never assume someone was guilty. And what
did I do? I assumed. I accused. I goofed.

You know who else was right? I hate to
admit it <grrrrr> but Aimee was right. She
said all along that I was getting kind of
obsessed with the whole detective scene.
She said it wasn't making me see things
clearly.

159

I already sent Penelope like six e-mails apologizing. She hasn't responded. She must think I'm a twit.

If I were an ostrich I could bury my head in the sand. But we don't have much sand in Far Hills.

What am I supposed to do now?

Madison looked up from her laptop. She'd barricaded herself up in the media lab at the library during Friday's lunch hour. The early classes of the day had gone by without much mention of the sheet music. But by lunchtime, the entire school was whispering about Mr. Olivetti's mistake.

Madison was too embarrassed about what she had said and done to face people at lunch. She couldn't deal with Egg and Chet's heckling, Dan's questions, and Aimee's "I told you so." And she was definitely too ashamed to look Hart in the eye.

It was better to hide out until things blew over, Madison told herself.

"There you are!"

Madison turned around. Fiona stood with her bag slung over one shoulder. In her hands were an orange, a container of yogurt, and a package of cheese and crackers.

"I knew you'd come up here. You always do. I smuggled these out of the cafeteria," Fiona said. "I heard about the mystery. I heard that Mr. Olivetti never had anything stolen. I figured you didn't want to talk about what happened. You must be so bummed."

"Bummed?" Madison said. "*Mortified* is more like it."

"How could you have known?" Fiona asked. "You only followed the leads like a real detective would. Like Major DeMille, right?"

"Right." Madison shook her head. "Is everyone laughing at me behind my back?"

"No," Fiona said right away.

Madison made a face. She wasn't convinced. "*No one* is laughing?"

Fiona paused. "Okay, my brother made a few jokes. But he's king of the obnoxious, you know that."

"Uh-huh," Madison said. "What about Hart?" she asked.

Fiona shrugged. "Well . . . I don't know," she said softly.

Madison knew what *that* meant. It meant Hart was laughing a little, too, but Fiona was too nice to tell Madison the truth.

"Want to walk home today after school?" Fiona asked.

"Sure," Madison said.

She wished the end of the day were there already.

At the end of the school day, Madison waited by her locker for Fiona. She hoped she would see

Aimee, too, but she figured Aimee probably had dance class. Aimee always had dance class these days. Lately Aimee had been missing from many of their friends' usual gatherings. Madison figured that she was the reason why. After flunking her *Crime Time* experiment, was Madison now in danger of losing her friend?

The hallway was packed with kids pushing their way past other kids. Some boy with a hockey stick sent a book flying down the corridor like a puck. A teacher waving a notebook chased after two girls. A pack of boys dressed in black T-shirts, with their hands in the pockets of their jeans, skulked by the water fountain.

And then, through the crowd, Ivy and the drones appeared.

Madison turned her head away so she wouldn't be recognized and so that she wouldn't have to say anything to Ivy. But the enemy and her cohorts, of course, couldn't resist making a few cruel comments on their way.

"Hey, Madison," Ivy jeered. "How's Little Miss Detective?"

"I heard you blew it," Rose said.

"Yeah, you can't solve anything," Joanie added.

The three laughed in unison.

"Why don't you go crawl under a rock?" Madison snapped.

Ivy tossed her red hair and put on a pout. "Oh,

crybaby, what's wrong?" The drones laughed again.

"Everyone knows what happened. You can run, but you can't hide. . . ." Ivy taunted Madison.

Madison was speechless.

But then someone else spoke up.

"You heard her, Ivy. Crawl under a rock."

Madison's eyes bugged out. That was Hart talking.

"What did you say?" Ivy said with disbelief. She glared at Hart.

"Quit being so mean, Ivy," Hart said. "You're always being mean for no reason."

"No reason? I have a perfectly good reason," Ivy snapped.

Madison didn't say anything. Neither did the drones.

"Oh, yeah? What's your reason?" Hart asked.

Ivy was in shock. Everyone was. Not only was Hart standing up for Madison, but he was saying everything that Madison and her BFFs thought about the enemy. Madison felt her heart pound. She had liked Hart before, but now she was ready to burst with like. Madison wondered if this was what love was—a shock to the system.

Ivy had clearly run out of things to say. Without another moment's hesitation, she and the drones buzzed down the hall. Madison hoped that she would, in fact, go find some rock to crawl under.

"Thanks, Hart," Madison said.

"She had it coming, Finnster," Hart said.

Madison thought his eyes were twinkling, but she couldn't be sure. After everything that had happened at the movies on Wednesday, the last thing Madison would have expected was *this*.

The crackling voice over the loudspeaker announced a full roster of after-school activities. More kids rushed past.

"So . . ." Madison said.

"I heard about Mr. Olivetti," Hart said.

"Yeah . . . well . . . duh . . . I should have known," Madison said. "I'm no detective."

"I know you were wrong about the mystery, but don't feel bad. Everyone makes mistakes, right?" Hart said. "Even me."

Madison chuckled. "You sound like my dad," she said.

Madison's throat muscles clenched. What was she talking about? Her dad? This wasn't her dad. This was Hart, the Hunk. She bit her tongue so she wouldn't say anything else stupid.

"Er . . . see you around," Hart said nervously.

"Thanks again," Madison said. "Really."

Hart nodded. "Whatever," he said.

Madison wrapped her arms around herself as she watched him walk away. Then she knelt and distractedly picked at a stone that had gotten lodged inside the bottom of her sneaker.

"Maddie! Maddie!" Fiona appeared at last, running down the hall. "I got stuck with a teacher, and I couldn't leave. Sorry. Ready to go?"

Madison nodded. "He just saved me," she said.

"Huh?"

"Ivy came by. She attacked me. And he rescued me. It was like a movie or something," Madison explained.

"Huh?" Fiona said again. "Who saved you?"

"Hart," Madison said. Now, *her* eyes were twinkling.

Fiona giggled. "Hart?"

"Maybe this whole detective thing didn't turn out so bad, after all. Maybe it was all meant to happen the way it did so I could have that three minutes with Hart," Madison said.

"Oh, Maddie," Fiona said. "You make me laugh."

"That's me. A regular laugh riot," Madison said.

They walked out of the building together and headed for home.

Mom was very understanding when Madison explained to her what had happened with the school mystery. She ordered a pizza and drove to Freeze Palace for cherry ice-cream sundaes for Madison and her.

After dinner, Madison finished up her homework and went online. It was quiet for a Friday night. Usually, Madison and her friends made plans for the weekend or at least met up in chat rooms to gossip about the week. But no one had made plans at school or called Madison up to do anything.

Inside the e-mailbox, however, it was another story. Madison had a slew of e-mails from almost all of her friends—and Dad, too.

Dad had sent his love. He and Stephanie wanted to know how the mystery had turned out.

Madison wrote back, "It didn't." She'd fill them in on the details later.

Dan had sent an e-mail from the clinic. He told Madison to "hang in there." Madison realized what a good friend Dan was. He always had something supportive and nice to say.

Lindsay had sent an e-mail with an apology for starting Madison on the mystery in the first place. "It's all my fault," Lindsay wrote. "If I hadn't been so nosy . . ."

Madison hit REPLY and reassured her friend that it wasn't anyone's fault, but it was nice to know how much Lindsay cared.

Even Egg had sent Madison an e-mail, although his was filled more with jokes and jibes than with words of support. But Madison laughed. She realized that she couldn't just hang on forever to her failure to solve her first big mystery.

Her friends were there. With laughs or hugs, they would help.

An Insta-Message popped up in the corner of her screen.

```
<BalletGrl>: hey
```

It was Aimee.
Madison almost burst into tears.
She typed a quick reply.

```
<MadFinn>: hey back
```

They went into a private chat room.

```
<BalletGrl>: I'm sorry
<MadFinn>: what 4
<BalletGrl>: I wasn't a v.g. friend
<MadFinn>: did Fiona tell u
<BalletGrl>: about the mystery yes I
   heard
<MadFinn>: go ahead and say it
<BalletGrl>: say what
<MadFinn>: say you told me so
<BalletGrl>: I won't
<MadFinn>: I hate Major DeMille
<BalletGrl>: no u don't
<MadFinn>: u were right mysteries r a
   TOTAL waste of time
<BalletGrl>: it's only 1 mystery
<MadFinn>: I guess so how's dance
<BalletGrl>: TBPO it's just ok u were
   right 2
<MadFinn>: about what
<BalletGrl> I spend 2 much time on
   dance just like u were spending 2
```

much time on those mysties sorry I
cant spell tonite MYSTERIES
<MadFinn>: I guess we were both a
little obsessed 4 real huh?
<BalletGrl>: I'm sorry
<MadFinn>: me 2
<BalletGrl>: I miss u
<MadFinn>: me 2
<BalletGrl>: how's Hart??????????
<MadFinn>: what did Fiona tell u
<BalletGrl>: she said u guys r the
perfect couple
<MadFinn>: and what do u say
<BalletGrl>: wanna come over for a
sleepover right now
<MadFinn>: tonight? But it's almost 8
<BalletGrl>: ask ur mom
<MadFinn>: ok I'll ask her
<BalletGrl>: hurry up if u get here
by 830 we can watch Crime Time
<MadFinn>: no way I'm over that show
<BalletGrl>: ok we can do other stuff
and just talk I really want to
hear what happened with Hart and
Mr. O and all that
<MadFinn>: ok well I better go then
<BalletGrl>: hurry up
<MadFinn>: i'll call if mom says no
<BalletGrl>: she won't
<MadFinn>: c u soon
<BalletGrl>: LY4E

Madison logged off so she could throw her pajamas into a bag. She was positive Mom would let her go over to Aimee's. They'd been sleeping over at each other's houses their whole lives.

Somehow, however, that night's sleepover felt a little different for Madison.

That night, Madison had gotten her friend back when she needed her most of all. And she wasn't going to let go, not for *Crime Time* or any mystery.

This time, all the evidence pointed to one very clear thing: she and Aimee were going to remain friends for a long time.

Mad Chat Words:

`:-(((`	Boo-hoo-hoo
`:-S`	It makes no sense
`:-{}`	Lip gloss kiss
`INYH`	I need your help
`B(2)`	Be square
`TM`	Trust me
`ML`	More later
`J/W`	Just wondering
`UR2N2ME`	You are too nice to me
`V.G.`	Very good
`4get`	Forget
`QW`	Quit worrying
`LY4E`	Love you forever

Madison's Computer Tip

I use my laptop for practically everything these days, but it was truly indispensable for trying to solve mysteries. **Use a computer document to make lists and keep track of pals and enemies.** My own personal Crime Time files really helped me keep up with all the facts of the case, especially when the facts kept changing! I could track all of my suspects with a click of the key, and THAT was very cool. I wonder how much Major DeMille uses his laptop!

Sign up for a Madison Finn newsletter at www.lauradower.com